"What In T

Jody blinked and sat bolt upright.

A redheaded woman had appeared at the foot of his bed. Backing away, she stumbled over his shoes.

"I certainly hope you're Jody Branigan. It's Friday afternoon, and I know I'm in the right hotel room," she stated.

In the split second it took his mind to clear he remembered, looked for something to put on and did what was characteristic of all five Branigan brothers. He rose from the bed without an ounce of false modesty.

"Megan O'Connor?"

She, too, was cool. "Considering your attire, I assume you were expecting someone else." After giving him one audacious glance from head to toe, she closed her eyes and held out his shirt.

Jody took the shirt from her outstretched hand. She had an arresting voice, not quite husky, mellow enough to make him want to hear more of it.

"In three months you and I will be family. That should allow you to throw me my pants."

Dear Reader:

It's October and there's no stopping our men! October's *Man of the Month* comes from the pen of Leslie Davis Guccione, whose books about the Branigan brothers have pleased countless readers. Mr. October is Jody Branigan, and you can read all about him in *Branigan's Touch*.

Coming in November is *Shiloh's Promise* by BJ James. You might remember Shiloh from his appearance in *Twice in a Lifetime*. We received so much positive feedback about this mesmerizing man that we knew he had to have his very own story—and that he'd make a perfect *Man of the Month*!

Needless to say, I think each and every Silhouette Desire is wonderful. October and November's books are guaranteed to give you hours of reading pleasure.

Enjoy!

Lucia Macro
Senior Editor

LESLIE
DAVIS
GUCCIONE

BRANIGAN'S TOUCH

SILHOUETTE *Desire*

Published by Silhouette Books New York

America's Publisher of Contemporary Romance

Jody's story is for all my readers
who took the time to tell me
how much they love the Branigans.

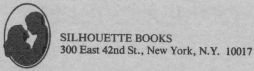

SILHOUETTE BOOKS
300 East 42nd St., New York, N.Y. 10017

ISBN: 0-373-05523-4

First Silhouette Books printing October 1989

Printed in the U.S.A.

Books by Leslie Davis Guccione

Silhouette Desire

Before the Wind #279
*Bittersweet Harvest #311
*Still Waters #353
*Something in Common #376
*Branigan's Touch #523

*Branigan Brothers

LESLIE DAVIS GUCCIONE

lives with her husband and three children in a state of semichaos in a historic sea captains' district south of Boston. When she's not at her typewriter she's actively researching everything from sailboats to cranberry bogs. What free time she has is spent sailing and restoring her circa-1827 Cape Cod cottage. Her ideas for her books come from the world around her. As she states, ''Romance is right under your nose.'' She has also written under the name Leslie Davis.

BRANIGAN FAMILY TREE

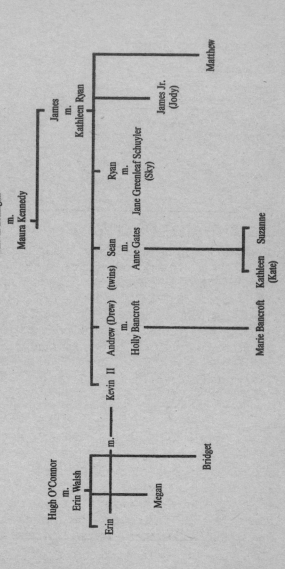

Kevin Branigan
m.
Maura Kennedy

Hugh O'Connor
m.
Erin Walsh

Kevin II

Erin

Megan

Bridget

Andrew (Drew)   (twins)   Sean
m.   m.
Holly Bancroft   Anne Gates

James
m.
Kathleen Ryan

Ryan
m.
Jane Greenleaf Schuyler
(Sky)

James Jr.
(Jody)

Matthew

Marie Bancroft

Kathleen   Suzanne
(Kate)

Prologue

Charm the daylights out of her.''

Jody Branigan looked at his oldest brother who was sitting next to him on the couch. "Kevin, according to you, Megan O'Connor's immune to Branigan charm. Besides, my week in New York will be frantic. I won't have time for anything but the seminars."

"Jody, I heard that." The voice came through the telephone receiver he held at his ear. Erin O'Connor, Kevin's fiancée, was on the line. "My sister thinks I'm throwing my life away but that's only because she doesn't know your family or Millbrook the way I do. If you agree to talk to her, Megan'll see another side and she'll realize there's more to all of you than just a family cranberry business. Give her the interview she wants for her radio station—she can even come to your hotel room. You won't have to do more than chat into a little microphone.''

Erin was sick with the flu and calling from her carriage-house apartment. Miserable though she sounded, Jody had no trouble discerning the determination in her voice as she continued, ''An in-depth public service program on wetlands protection with someone of your caliber would be a real feather in her cap.''

''And out of gratitude, she'll suddenly think your marrying Kevin is the right thing after all? Come on, Erin! Besides, I'll barely have time. If I see her, won't she expect dinner or a drink someplace? She'll probably feel obliged to show me the town.''

''You might like a night on the town with Megan.''

''Erin—''

''Okay, okay. Interview only. An hour into her microphone. I'll get her to swear to it. Be your irresistible self and expound on the sterling qualities of your eldest brother.''

''Haven't you done that already?''

''Megan needs a second opinion, preferably male. Yours.''

Jody grimaced and looked at Kevin.

''Melt her heart, kid,'' Kevin said.

''I don't know anything about melting hearts.''

''Baloney.'' That was from Erin. ''Heart-melting is a genetic trait in your family. Talk business. Give her the interview. One of you is bound to mention the bride and groom up here on the bogs. When the subject comes up, do your stuff. She's really very lovable. Misguided, but lovable.''

''Fine,'' he sighed. ''Tell her late Friday, four-thirty or five o'clock. It's the best I can do.'' He felt hardhearted. ''Get well while I'm gone.''

His schedule was frantic enough without explaining the ins and outs of groundwater supplies, aquifers and commercial development to a disapproving, neophyte public service director for an out-of-the-way New Jersey radio station, family or not. But he'd agreed to it.

One

A week later, Jody Branigan stood on the Wall Street sidewalk and let the sharp April wind sting his face, trying to shake some of the fatigue that dogged him. What he longed for was a room with a bed. A firm mattress, cool, clean sheets and the perfect pillow had as much appeal at that moment as any fantasy, be it woman, meal or desert island.

His head was buzzing with information culled from the five days of legal symposia. Friday's meetings were over early, however, and even before his hired limousine had moved into the traffic, he'd unbuttoned his starched white collar and pulled the club tie away from his throat.

Jody had clear, green eyes and a tough, no-nonsense expression that could be softened by a devastating smile. Nut-colored hair topped six feet of perfectly proportioned body. His lean, muscular build didn't come from the gym workouts his associates assiduously attended but from the demanding physical labor on his brothers' cranberry bogs. At twenty-nine, James D. Branigan, Jr., Esq., looked like Hollywood's idea of a district attorney from a homicide division.

He was, however, an environmental lawyer, one of the younger members of Hammell, Price and Bennett, Attorneys-at-Law, a prestigious Massachusetts firm located in Plymouth. On any given workday, Jody was apt to juggle crises from local lobstermen to the ramifications of beach erosion to Cape Cod.

Manhattan was light-years from the small-town pace of Plymouth or even the Yankee reserve of Boston, but it was where the best minds had come together to discuss the increasing problem of wetlands protection. He'd carved a week out of his already-crowded agenda to attend the sessions and his briefcase bulged with the work he still had to do. The end-of-the-day gesture of tugging his tie from his collar was managed with one hand, while he toted his legal work with the other.

He entered his hotel, giving a cursory nod to the uniformed doorman, and fished his room key from his pocket. Without bothering to stop at the desk, he stepped onto the elevator and punched his floor, berating himself for ever having accepted Preston Eldridge's dinner invitation. Not that there'd been a choice.

As the steel doors slid shut, Jody ate the last of his antacids. Eldridge was senior partner of the firm hosting the seminars and a leading expert in the field. Being wined and dined by him was a perk impossible to turn down, and one which made Jody desperate for a catnap. He'd need all his wits at dinner if he were to add anything to the verbal menu.

Jody got off the elevator and walked the empty hall. It was four-fifteen in the afternoon and even allowing for a shower and shave, he had time to swallow a couple aspirin and catch a decent nap before Eldridge's limousine arrived to take him to dinner at six.

In less time than it takes to pack a courtroom, he'd stripped to his shorts, draped his shirt and suit on the hard-backed chair and stretched his six-foot frame across the bed. Time and work pressures were temporarily suspended. He lay on his back, his eyes closed, a shock of hair across his forehead. As he drifted, he reviewed the day's work, decided what he'd wear to dinner and promptly fell asleep.

A sixth sense tugged Jody from his deep, dreamless sleep. Groggy, he blinked once and then shock brought him bolt upright. A redheaded woman had appeared at the foot of his bed. Backing away, she stumbled over his shoes and seemed determined to focus on them rather than the expanse of male pulchritude draped across the bed in front of her.

"What the hell?"

"I certainly hope you're Jody Branigan. It's Friday afternoon and I know I'm in the right hotel room," she replied.

The interview! In the split second it took for his mind to clear, Jody remembered, looked for something to put on, and did what was characteristic of all five Branigan brothers. He rose from the bed without an ounce of false modesty. The shock to his system had already registered, however, and he couldn't stop the blush that was rapidly spreading across his face.

"Megan O'Connor?"

She, too, was cool. "Considering your attire, I assume you've forgotten our interview or were, perhaps, expecting someone else." She took his dress shirt from the back of the chair and held it out to him at arm's length. After giving one audacious glance from head to toe, she closed her eyes. "I suppose I should make a pun about a lawyer and his briefs, but I'm at a loss for words."

"Hardly an O'Connor trait," Jody replied as he took the shirt from her outstretched hand. How could he have forgotten the damned interview! "Megan, I'm sorry. It's been a busy week."

"And you forgot all about me."

While his complexion cooled he buttoned his shirt.

"I should be insulted, Counselor," she said mildly.

Jody buttoned the cuffs. She had an arresting voice, not quite husky, just mellow enough to make him want to hear more of it. "Erin will think this is hilarious when she gets wind of it. You've taken it in stride, just as she would have."

Megan opened one eye. "My sister's a nurse. There's not a lot we have in common."

"So I understand. In three months you and I will be family. That should allow you to throw me my pants."

"Would you like me to wait in the hall till you're decent?"

He laughed. "I'd say the damage was done. Just hand me my pants."

Megan handed them over. She was looking at the floor, but without any air of embarrassment. "You do recall agreeing to this interview?"

"Your presence at the end of my bed has jogged my memory."

"I called this morning and left a reminder message at the desk."

"Which I missed." As he buttoned and belted his pants, Jody watched her, still magnetized by her voice. She was in broadcasting; that was the explanation. It seemed a lifetime ago that he'd agreed to the favor.

His lack of enthusiasm coupled with the rigors of his week had driven the whole conversation out of his head. In fact, he hadn't so much as speculated on what this O'Connor might look like, which only proved how exhausted he was.

It didn't matter. Speculation wouldn't have done her justice. She was a glorious redhead. He would have expected a sprite, a perky little thing like Erin, but with the exception of the blue eyes, this O'Connor was a different species altogether.

In place of the country freshness he associated with Erin, there was sophistication, a self-confident sparkle. Megan's hair was fiery red, with the vibrancy of a sunset, worn pulled off one temple with a tortoiseshell comb.

She appeared to be about her sister's height, but even under the jacket and skirt of her linen suit, it was obvious that her figure was fuller. As he finished dressing, Megan slipped off her blazer and put it where his shirt had been. Her peach silk blouse billowed, then clung as she moved, making her seem suddenly soft, unconsciously seductive.

Jody bent for his socks and found himself glancing from her hem to her ankles and back. His physical response to her was as big a shock as her entrance. He decided to leave his shirttail out.

This was Megan, the O'Connor determined to succeed, the one who unceremoniously put the family farm behind her and pushed full steam ahead. The one who thought anyone marrying back into a farming family was wasting her life. "Megan's a lot like you," Erin had said on more than one occasion to Jody, "onward and upward."

As Jody dressed, he hastily culled fragments of what Erin had told him about her. The O'Connor sisters had been reared on a dairy farm in western New Jersey. Although Megan hadn't grown up far from the city in terms of miles, it had been light years from the sophistication that she now embraced. Megan, apparently, never tired of the bustle and excitement implicit in Manhattan.

Work in communications for a major radio network was part of her dream. Geographically, her position at Hackettstown's WHNJ hadn't put her much closer to New York City, but after only two years, she'd risen to Public Service Director.

There were undeniable similarities to his own situation—but there was an enormous difference, too, which Jody never mentioned when Erin brought it up. Megan's upwardly mobile drive was self-motivated. Leaving the Branigan cranberry bogs, which were his heritage, was nothing Jody had done by choice.

His professional future had been mapped out by his oldest brother Kevin, and the late Peter Bancroft, their bog manager, and neighbor, who, in the wake of the accidental death of the Branigan parents had become the six orphaned brothers' guardian. To question where Jody was in life was to open a Pandora's box better left firmly shut.

Once in his pants, Jody sat down on the edge of the bed and rubbed the day's stubble on his chin as he looked at her. "I apologize. This is all my fault."

"Yes it is. You've put me in an embarrassing position."

Her tone made him look at her again, or maybe it was curiosity that had him staring. "You could have knocked."

"I would have, but my note hadn't been picked up at the desk, and I assumed you were still out."

"Megan, I've apologized. A favor to your sister is hardly on the top of my agenda."

"A favor, is that how you see this?"

He raised his hand. "Forgive me. I'm half asleep." He glanced at his watch. "I'm sorry I fouled things up. It's all my fault but there's just no time for the interview. Maybe we can reschedule this. Perhaps at the wedding in July?"

"Reschedule? Jody, I've come all the way in—" Megan stopped, as if fearing she'd sound unprofessional. "We can't reschedule."

"We'll have to. As I recall, you wanted an hour's worth of information to break into two thirty-minute segments. I've got a dinner appointment in less time than that."

"Break it."

He did his best not to sound incredulous. "That's impossible."

"Delay it. That's reasonable." Megan sat down on the hard-backed chair and crossed her legs. "I should think your first obligation is to this commitment. Be late to dinner."

"Excuse me?"

"Obviously, Attorney Branigan, you haven't given this more than a minute's thought. However, I've planned an entire month's focus around the issues you'll be discussing with me. Please be reasonable.

WHNJ is giving this an additional evening slot as well as the usual noon broadcast. What I cull from an hour with you will be the basis for the program. You don't really think I'd let you slip through my fingers because you forgot and now it's too close to your dinner date!''

Jody replied evenly, "It's a working dinner with experts in wetlands protection and a lawyer from the Environmental Protection Agency. Not my idea of a date, frankly."

"So when do you leave town?" she asked.

"I'm taking the 9:00 a.m. shuttle."

"Newark to Boston?"

Jody nodded. "Put this off. I'll give you twice as much time when you're in Millbrook."

"Can't."

So much for heart-melting. "Then accept my apology. That's the best I can do."

"Meet with me tomorrow morning, before breakfast, before you leave."

"Impossible."

Megan uncrossed her legs and glanced at the bed. "You'll be having company tonight, after your working dinner?"

Jody's response was a sort of defeated chuckle. Steely determination stiffened his spine, but his Irish features were drawn in a combination of fatigue and grit. His penetrating gaze softened as he suddenly, boyishly, rubbed his hazel eyes with the back of his fist.

Megan stood up and put out her hand. "We'll make it business after pleasure. You have fun after your dinner tonight and I'll be back at seven in the morning. We can meet in the lobby so I don't disturb your guest and I'll still be able to make my deadline. Though, it'll cost me an arm and a leg to get a room in this town." She snapped her fingers. "How's your expense account? This is a PR venture for you and your firm."

He reached out, not to shake her hand but tug her back into her chair. "Slow down. You're jumping to conclusions."

She cocked her head. "Over your love life or my request that your law firm consider picking up my tab?"

He raised his eyebrows and said, "Both."

"Empty bed and no expense account. Don't you dare suggest I stay here and save the money."

"Never crossed my mind," he mused. Sparring, sexual or otherwise, was exhausting, and they were getting off the subject.

Megan picked up a pen and wagged it at him. "You've put my project in jeopardy, Jody. I couldn't care less who you sleep with, but I don't appreciate being swept aside like some inconsequential, neophyte reporter because it doesn't suit your schedule."

He flushed and the betrayal of his complexion made him swear.

"The truth will out," Megan snapped, "and it appears to be embarrassing you."

"Megan, my 'date' tonight is with Preston Eldridge—the keynote speaker at lunch."

She perked up. "Preston Eldridge who represented the Warren County Conservation Commission in the Allamuchy Reservoir suit?"

"You've done some research, I gather."

"Of course," she scoffed. "That's my listeners' neck of the woods. I'm loaded with thought-provoking, pertinent questions."

"So I've noticed." Damn, but her eyes were blue.

Megan poked the air with the pen. "Eating with the EPA and no overnight guest? I have a better idea—take me to dinner with you."

It must have been the fatigue; Jody found himself actually considering her suggestion.

"Unless you think you'll embarrass me and fall asleep in your vichyssoise," she was saying, looking over at him rather skeptically.

Jody yawned. "There's always that chance."

Two

She smiled. "I really do appreciate the chance to interview you, of course, but a meal with Preston Eldridge suggests endless possibilities."

Jody suffered the damnedest feeling that he'd just been passed over for someone better. "Megan, you aren't invited."

"Any spouses or whomevers going along? You might as well tell me the truth. The way you blush makes lying useless."

How well he knew. "Guests were mentioned and the woman from the EPA is with her husband. Don't look so triumphant."

"I could pass for your whomever."

It must have been the fatigue. This impossible creature was not only wearing down what little resistance he had, her innocent innuendos were conjuring up images that made his pulse race. It was the blouse. When she moved, the lamplight flowed across the soft silky curves as if it were liquid. Megan O'Connor, liquid lamplight. He was far too tired.

Jody walked to the window without answering. City lights were on and far below, the street was thick with rush-hour traffic. He pulled the draperies closed and turned on another lamp.

"I'll be a fly on the wall," she was saying. "Dinner with Preston and your associates, then we'll come back here to your room for a quick interview after dinner—"

"We won't come back to my room," came quickly.

"Then in the lobby. I'll interview you downstairs and be on my way tonight, out of your hair."

Fat chance popped into his head.

"You won't have to give me a second thought until Erin's wedding rehearsal. What do you think?"

"You can't go to dinner as my date and then prod the lawyers all night with intelligent questions."

"Was there a compliment in there?"

"Possibly," he muttered.

Megan waited.

Jody looked again at her expectant, confident expression. It might be interesting to see her in action. "All right, I'll call and see what I can do. I owe you that much."

"Thank you, Jody."

"You may not look like your sister, but you've got the O'Connor perseverance."

There was warmth in Megan's smile. "Erin's always gone after what she wanted. She taught me everything I know about determination, though from what Kevin's told me, you and I are pretty evenly matched in that department."

"I wouldn't have gotten very far without it."

"Neither would I." Megan put her jacket back on, which gave Jody an excuse to watch her move. Liquid light. Extraordinary.

Megan used Jody's bathroom to freshen up while he called the Eldridge penthouse to get her included at dinner, and when Jody explained her project, he was assured of cooperation. It was as simple as asking; he didn't know whether he was glad or not.

Megan emerged with fresh makeup and restyled hair, then agreed to meet Jody in the lobby after he had a chance to shower and shave.

"I haven't left you much time to catch that nap," she added as he opened the door to the hall.

"No, you haven't." Her apologetic expression stirred a modicum of guilt and he softened, adding, "I'll manage."

"Yes, I thought you might."

He fought the urge to watch her walk to the elevator and closed the door.

Once again, he took off his clothes and lay back on the bed, thinking about Megan's presence at dinner. It would be interesting.

Jody tried to doze but the thought of her standing at the foot of the bed watching him kept him from nodding off. He saw her surprise and the faint amusement in her eyes. He'd have to make sure he told his brothers the anecdote before Megan described it to Erin. Stories like this circulated for months before they were laid to rest.

Had she blushed, as well? His life was layered with responsibilities and complications and the vision of a woman instead of pressing legal work should have been refreshing and relaxing. But she was the wrong woman.

Under her polished exterior he'd glimpsed a will of iron. Megan was vibrant, maybe even volatile. Jody wanted neither arguments nor personal entanglements with her. Either extreme seemed distinctly possible, but she'd be family soon, someone you couldn't say goodnight to and not worry about seeing again.

He cursed and left the bed for the bathroom, but even over the menthol of his shaving cream, the mirrored space still smelled provocatively of her perfume. Traces filled his head and he stared hard at his reflection. Descriptions, bits and pieces of her, surfaced from his memory. The sister so often described by Erin was taking on decidedly human characteristics. If ever a woman needed to be kept at arm's length, it was Megan O'Connor.

Precisely on time, Jody emerged from the elevator bank and walked across the hotel lobby. He'd changed from the day's white to a light blue dress shirt and his suit was the same impeccable charcoal gray.

Megan was sitting on an upholstered bench by a potted ficus plant and rose as she caught sight of him. He looked striking in clothes...or out of them, this attorney fresh off the cranberry bogs of southern Massachusetts, Megan thought, then strove for professionalism. "I checked my tape recorder at the desk, but I've brought a small notepad. This could prove to be a very interesting evening," she said. "I'm looking forward to it."

"Make the best of it," he replied.

"Of course." She cocked her head. "You look nice and rested. In fact, you're quite impressive."

"I'm glad you approve."

Her laugh was rich, confident. "Branigans don't need my approval."

Jody touched her elbow and led her across the lobby to the exit. "They don't deserve your disapproval."

"My reputation precedes me," she murmured. "Have I been too hard on the Branigans?"

"Your sister's marrying my brother and she cares very much what you think."

"She's discussed this with you?"

Jody looked straight ahead. "Family matters tend to get discussed among the family members. My brothers are a close-knit bunch."

"You don't sound as if you're including yourself."

Jody shrugged. He was willing to talk about Kevin and Erin. His own situation was not open for discussion. He neither needed nor wanted her comments.

Megan knew of Millbrook and the Branigan cranberry bogs only from her sister's descriptions, but she hadn't been able to hold back her opinion that marrying a cranberry grower and settling down in the sand flats of New England was hardly different from the cows and corn in the O'Connor background. Where was the appeal in that? Megan had asked Erin more than once.

"Regardless of how I feel about Erin and Kevin, I hope you know that I appreciate this, Jody," Megan was saying.

He looked at her. "From what I've seen when a Branigan runs up against an O'Connor, compromise saves a great deal of teeth gnashing."

Megan laughed and the sound of it danced deliciously along his spine, provocatively enough so that a caution sign flashed in his head. The sensation only intensified as she brushed against him. The doorman ushered them out and Jody was grateful for the snap in the night air.

"Let's make the most of this evening," Megan said, as if she were oblivious to the effect she had on him.

Preston Eldridge's driver and limousine were at the curb. As they got into the back seat, Megan whispered, "You did tell Eldridge that I'm in communications? He won't think I'm just your whomever?"

"You're not my whomever type."

"Good." Megan patted his knee in an irritatingly sisterly way as they settled into the plush seat, and the sleek black car inched into the traffic. "Some day you'll have to tell me what your type is. Right now I want to know how the Clean Water Act will affect the proposed development in Warren County."

Jody had only to turn his head in order to look right into her striking and ever-inquisitive face. "The deal was dinner. Not another word until we get there." He put his head back, and for the duration of the ride, sat with his eyes closed, inhaling the stimulating fragrance of a newly cooperative Megan. In the silence, he recalled what he knew about her, constructing a three-dimensional personality the way he might build a legal case from depositions and interrogatories.

At twenty-four, Megan was out to make her reputation. She was the middle of three sisters, but her simple roots and the O'Connor dairy farm in Deans Corner, New Jersey, were something of an embarrassment, a way of life to be put behind her.

She was bright. Jody knew she'd been a scholarship student at an exclusive Somerset County boarding school. He also knew it bothered Erin that Megan had adopted the trappings, the upper class speech, wardrobe and view of life that had surrounded her during those impressionable years.

By the time she'd entered her freshman year in college, Megan Katherine O'Connor had perfected a privileged attitude about money, goals, life in general and especially men. With his eyes still closed, Jody smiled. The attitude was evident in her walk, her wit and the very fact that she now sat next to him in the back seat of Preston Eldridge's limousine.

In Millbrook Erin had laughingly and lovingly compared her own demanding but simple and quiet life to her sister's Manhattan nights, Southampton summers and Vermont winter weekends. Jody opened his eyes and looked at Megan's face as they inched through the traffic. Had Megan ever found herself out of her league?

They arrived and were met by the rest of the party at the door. Maison Provence was an Upper East Side restaurant that epitomized Megan's idea of haute cuisine as well as haute clientele. A meal would cost her a month's salary and a seat was a minor miracle, but for the league she was in tonight, it was business as usual. Megan's presence brought the seating to seven: Jody, Eldridge and his younger associate, David Howell, two EPA lawyers, one spouse and herself.

As they followed the maître d', Megan took Jody's arm. He watched her glance once around the room. Captains of industry and Wall Street weren't usually recognizable; still there was no doubt as to the caliber of the company.

They were shown a rear table, secluded enough for conversation. As the evening progressed, Megan came into her own. After Jody's introduction and the usual pleasantries, she led a discussion on county issues that both Eldridge and Howell debated. She asked pointed, intelligent questions, flattering the group when necessary, taking notes with their approval.

Megan was seated on Jody's left with David Howell on the other side, and Jody kept an ear on the conversation that blossomed between them. Even after a full day of work, Megan was charged with energy, pressing David with the same focus and enthusiasm she'd used on Jody in the hotel room. Though they discussed only business, their intensity engendered a sense of intimacy Megan seemed to do nothing to dispel.

They stopped talking only when the dessert cart was wheeled to the table. Everyone indulged, and with sweets and coffee, conversation became general and the evening ended with anecdotes and humor rather than business.

Two limousines had been hired to accommodate the group and they separated at the curb. Megan, Jody and David accompanied Preston in his, while the EPA group left in the other.

Megan insisted on taking the jump seat and sat facing the three men as they were driven back downtown. Jody was quiet, grateful that the day was nearly over. The evening's wine, the *boeuf bourguignonne* and the mousse were soporific and he marveled at the energy still emanating from the redhead across from him.

She exuded confidence and enthusiasm, and what could have been arrogance was tempered by wit. She'd breathed life into what had promised to be one more dry business meal. From her body language to the music in her laugh, her message was clear: Megan O'Connor had the world on a string.

Jody wasn't the only one marveling. David Howell had given her an evening's worth not only of his infallible opinions but also his undivided attention.

Howell was old money, Upper East Side stock, slick, surefooted, fast-track and obviously intrigued. Jody watched the city lights undulate over Megan as they drove. She laughed at something David said and turned her face to the window. Lamplight again.

She was Howell's type: smart as a whip, with a wide-eyed enthusiasm that masked the aggression her profession demanded. She'd held her own all night—in fact she'd led the way. Since she'd asked the questions and offered nothing personal, she was still an enigma.

Jody's mind wandered. How involved did Megan let herself get with men? Jody continued to watch her as she spoke. He thought about her pointed, even sexy repartee of the afternoon. He imagined her surprising David Howell on the bed in his underwear. His gut tightened and he blamed it on the meal because the idea that it might be concern or—heaven forbid—jealousy was clearly ridiculous.

Three

Preston Eldridge's limousine pulled up to the hotel curb. Over the ensuing thank yous to his host, comments on the past week and wishes for a safe flight back to Boston, Jody got out of the car.

When Megan emerged, it was with David in tow. Jody's disposition darkened as he waited. Megan carefully explained the reason for her presence at the hotel, mentioning the upcoming interview *in the lobby*. She and David exchanged business cards.

It was close to 11:00 p.m. and when the wind sliced through Jody he stuffed his hands into his pockets. They said something to each other he couldn't hear and finally, David got back into the limousine.

Megan and Jody crossed the lobby and she got her tape recorder from the desk. "You've hardly said a word since dinner. You look exhausted." She touched his arm. "I know you're dead on your feet. This is no way to get a decent interview. Frankly, talking to David opened so many new options I'm rethinking this whole project."

"Megan, I said I'd give you the interview."

"Oh, I intend to get it, later. Can we go to your room first, before you fall asleep standing up?"

Go to my room? Jody looked at her riveting blue eyes.

When he didn't reply, she smiled. "Remember? Upstairs, number seven seventeen." She started for the elevator.

He followed and leaned heavily against the wall as she pushed the button. "Megan, your modus operandi needs a little discussion."

"You don't really want to sit in the lobby. We'll go up. I think you can be trusted."

He sighed. "You hardly know me."

"Should I be afraid you'll make a pass at me? I know you don't want to muddy the Branigan-O'Connor waters any more than I do. You've already told me I'm not your type. In-laws shouldn't be. It's too complicated."

The elevator opened onto the seventh floor and he waited for her to step out into the hall. "Did I say that?"

"Yes, when we were discussing 'whomevers.' Of course I knew that anyway. I'm a good judge of character. With your agrarian background, I'm sure you like women more—*je ne sais quoi*—physical, less intellectual or goal oriented."

"Agrarian, as in working class."

"Yes, like my family. Don't take offense."

He unlocked his door and wondered if he looked offended. His fatigue was lifting temporarily. "You think Branigans are from the barefoot-and-pregnant school?''

Megan laughed as they went in. ''That's rather extreme for the eighties, but there's a certain attitude about women, a way of life, that our families maintain. My mother didn't go to college. She was happy tending to us. From what Kevin told me, your mother was the same. There are six of you, after all.''

Jody's memory of Kate Branigan was frozen in time, a child's perception of security. She had been a loving mother devoted to her family. ''If I admit to that, then you'll think you're right.''

''I'm not?''

''Have you met any of the Branigan women?''

''See? *The Branigan Women*. Even that categorizes them.''

''In the sense that they married and took on that surname, yes. Do you want me to apologize?''

''Heavens no. You are what you are, Jody. That handsome, sort of brawling cowboy attitude can be very alluring to your kind of female. I'm sure lots of women find you extremely sexy.''

Jody sat down on the edge of the bed. ''Thank you—I think. I'm not sure my sisters-in-law would thank you, however. We Branigans try very hard not to brawl.''

''Matt and Kevin got into a fist fight over Erin. Fourth of July, wasn't it?''

''I think she was flattered.''

''She wasn't any such thing! She thought the whole episode was sophomoric.''

''Love can do that to you,'' Jody replied solely to watch her response.

''Love? Blinded by infatuation is more like it.''

Jody avoided specifics. "You don't like us much, do you? You think life at the bogs will swallow little Erin right up."

"You're teasing."

"Perhaps you deserve it." He yawned, making no attempt to hide it. "You haven't met any of the Branigan women."

"Couldn't you just say, 'sisters-in-law'?"

"I could. Holly, Anne and Sky. Is that better?"

"Yes. Of course I haven't met them. Not yet, but they do, after all, live and work around the bogs, giving all their emotional support to your brothers."

There wasn't an ounce of argument left in him. Megan O'Connor could think anything she damn well liked. In three months she'd be in Millbrook for the wedding and she could set herself straight. Not that he cared, of course. Someone else would have to do the heart-melting.

Anne, Holly, Sky and even Erin were as different from one another as the men they loved. Anne and Sean had been high-school sweethearts, married far longer than the others, but Anne had a brain and she used it.

Holly Bancroft Branigan had inherited the Bittersweet Bogs, which bordered theirs. She and Drew had developed them into a third of the Branigan interest and she'd worked right through her first pregnancy. Not only did she have a bachelor's degree, but she was pregnant again and intended to go back for her MBA after the birth of the baby.

And Sky? Jane Greenleaf Schuyler had been Sky Branigan since November. She was precisely the type of woman that Megan used as her role model. She had brought financial and social independence to her relationship with Ryan, and gave all of them a touch of class. It was part of what made her unique and kept Ryan intrigued.

Jody pulled off his tie. "Is Erin making a mistake?"

Megan sat down in the chair and kicked off her shoes. "She doesn't think so."

"You'd never convince a jury with that tone of voice."

"Erin's doing the convincing. What's right for her isn't necessarily right for me."

"Then it's a darn good thing I didn't bring you up here to propose marriage." Desire stirred in him and he reminded himself that he hadn't brought her to his room to propose anything.

She looked startled. "You're making fun of me again."

Ever the lawyer, Jody let instinct lead the way. "Sometimes, Megan, you ask for it. No, I won't propose. You're holding out for a David Howell type."

Anger mottled her complexion and she blushed furiously. "I am not *holding out* for anyone!" At her being caught off guard, her eyes widened.

He'd expected a witty retort, a consummate professional stiff with indignation. Instead she seemed to soften and for a moment she was all peach silk, pink cheeks and flaming hair. It threw him off guard, too, and a rush of desire seized him so strongly, he was glad he was seated. She turned away and he determined to keep the focus on her, lest he give himself away.

"My, my," he mused, enjoying her embarrassment, "You're so sure about your observations, I just thought I'd throw in a few of my own."

"I resent it. I'm here professionally. Please keep your inaccurate personal observations to yourself." Composure intact, Megan's voice had regained its dismissive tone.

"Then let's dispense with the small talk and get on with business. Have you gotten a room for tonight?"

"No. I'll be honest."

"Are you ever anything else?"

Megan glared. "Will you let me finish?"

"I wish you would, but please don't tell me you were planning to camp out in here tonight." He yawned again, not daring to indulge in the pleasures of thinking about what he'd just suggested.

"I need you to come with me." She came across the room and sat next to him on the bed. "You're dog tired. I think a simple interview is beyond you right now. Besides, I've decided I want to expand this project. Spend the weekend with me. We'll do the interview tomorrow, which will give me time to rework my questions."

"Spend the weekend with you?"

"Yes." She was all business. "Check out of the hotel and stay with me. We can even go to the radio station for the interview. It'll make everything so much easier."

"Easier? For whom?"

She sighed. "Tonight I learned that David Howell knows all about the issues affecting my local audience. You, however, know all about the regional implications in coastal Massachusetts. Jody, our affiliate station is in that area."

"Why is that so important? You've got Howell now. You've got everything you need for New Jersey. Forget me."

"I can't! It's imperative that I use you so they see what I can do." Megan blushed.

"See what you can do?"

"You're being very stubborn." She seemed to be rushing.

"All this so you can run the show on the Plymouth station, too?"

"Yes. Then I can double or triple my exposure."

He was intrigued but the caution light was now on permanently. He had deadlines waiting, paperwork and calls to return. Jody put his fingers against Megan's mouth to silence her and instantly regretted it. Her breath drifted down his palm and the ache in him was palpable. He removed his hand. "Forget it, Megan. I'm on my own timetable."

"Jody, I need this." Her voice was intoxicating in its sensuality, deliberate or otherwise. He couldn't remember the last time he'd argued with a woman he'd ached to hold instead. She touched his arm. "You've been patient—infuriating sometimes, but patient. Stay over and I promise you a good night's sleep. I'll drive you to Newark first thing Sunday and you can still be back home with the day ahead of you. It's only an hour."

"It's a lifetime."

"Say yes."

"Megan, I've got depositions waiting and a proposal to write for the bogs. I've been away from my desk for a week. I can't spare the time."

"Jody, there's more to this than you know. My job's at stake."

He paused. Her tone was compelling and there was a hint of desperation in her eyes.

"An interview with me will save it? Hardly a trump card."

"How can you be so unconcerned?"

"Professional distance."

Her voice tightened. "I'm serious."

"Then you'd better tell me what's going on. I'm dead on my feet and tired of being manipulated."

"Manipulating you is an exercise in futility."

"Then give it up and try the truth."

"All right! There's talk of a takeover. A communications network in the midwest is negotiating for the stations. I'm low man on the totem pole and if anybody goes, it'll be me. A program like this gives me credibility, Jody." Her voice fell half an octave and she touched his arm. "Please help me."

He looked right into her eyes. Her embarrassment of moments earlier was gone. Her voice, her soft, sensuous plea was a contradiction to her determination and somehow she'd wrapped him in all of it.

It was the contradictions that stirred him. She was the personification of challenge. What would it take to recall the vulnerability she'd inadvertently let him glimpse. A kiss? She'd fight out of principle if nothing else.

"Please," she reiterated. "I'll never ask you for another thing. Not ever."

"Why does that sound familiar?"

"It wouldn't kill you to agree."

"That remains to be seen."

Megan stood up. "I should have known. You Branigans are all too stubborn! All right, then, come sit by the desk. Call room service and have them send up some coffee. This'll take a little over an hour, which puts us at close to two in the morning—after which time you'll have to walk me three blocks to the parking garage."

"I'll walk you to the elevator across the hall."

"No, you're too much of a gentleman to let me go alone at this hour. You'll see me to my car and then stay awake half the night fretting that I'll fall asleep at the wheel on my way home."

"When did you draw that conclusion?"

"It runs in your family."

Jody gathered his strength and crossed to his suitcase, thinking as he went that perhaps she knew as much about him as he knew about her. The thought was unsettling. He pulled out a fresh T-shirt and tossed it to her. "I'm not walking anybody anywhere. Strip down and put this on."

"That's ridiculous."

"So's your suggestion. If you want the interview, you can sleep here, on that side of the bed, and we'll talk in the morning. You can put the tape recorder between us. I'm not going anywhere and I'm too tired to behave as anything but a perfect gentleman. We can wake up at six, if need be. I'll talk and then you can get out of here. I'll still make my plane and I can get home in time to strangle your sister for suggesting the interview and my brother for—" He stopped.

She waited. "For what? You're the color of shrimp."

"Nothing."

"I don't want to know. Not if it came from one of your brawling brothers." She, too, was a shade darker and they stared at each other for a moment that could only be called pregnant.

"He told me to melt your heart," Jody finally murmured. "Erin seems to think she needs your blessing."

Megan was flustered. "I only worry for her own good." She held the shirt at the shoulders, between her thumbs and forefingers. As if forcing herself back on track, she shook it out. "You can't be serious. This is certainly not what I had in mind!"

"Neither is a weekend in New Jersey what I have in mind! Take it or leave it. It's the best I can do."

Megan straightened her shoulders. "Just forget the whole thing. You go back to Boston. I'll rework my program. I can keep it local and substitute David Howell. I sincerely doubt that he'll throw his underwear at me and suggest that I share his bed."

Jody considered telling her not to be too sure and watched her toss his shirt back at the suitcase. She was still angry, but there was hurt in her eyes. He let her gather up her purse and straighten her skirt. "Is it true about the takeover at your station?"

"Do you think I made it up?"

"To win your case and get me to stay for the weekend? Possibly."

Now there was fight in her eyes and maybe a little amusement. She scoffed, "James Branigan, from the looks you've been giving me, it would simply have been a matter of unbuttoning my blouse to get you to stay for the weekend." Then she started for the door.

He choked out a laugh. "A beautiful woman in my hotel room, even one who means nothing but trouble, has put my imagination into overdrive."

It broke the ice and Megan laughed, too. "We should have stayed in the lobby."

What was one more day? For reasons far clearer to his hormonal system than his intellect, he stood up and said, "I'll go home with you."

Four

As it turned out, there was valet parking and the car was brought to the hotel. Megan's apology for her fib was perfunctory. In the course of the evening, something had happened between them that Jody was still reluctant to name. He was enjoying her. It wasn't intimacy, it was what his half-Italian sister-in-law Holly would call *sympatico*.

"Sleep," Megan had commanded as she drove him out of the city. He didn't last much beyond the George Washington Bridge. As they'd left the cityscape behind them, Jody had leaned back in the passenger seat and closed his eyes. By the time Megan drove them into New Jersey and reached the exit for Interstate 80, he was dead to the world.

Under the incandescent glow of the highway lights, his handsome face was full of changing shadows. He was at rest, but no one would describe him as peaceful. The Jody Branigan Megan had glimpsed in the past eight hours didn't seem at peace with much of anything, certainly not her, and not himself, either. His fatigue seemed as much mental as physical.

Interstate 80 was quiet and quite dark once they left the metropolitan area behind. It was well after midnight when Megan reached the Hackettstown exit and the interstate that wound through the Allamuchy Mountain range. As the road climbed, the valley fell away to the northeast, a spectacular view in the daylight. Even under the moon, the April night was full of the deep gray silhouettes of the pine forest. It was always a surprise to those who thought of the Garden State as nothing more than the belching industry hugging the New York skyline.

As Jody slept, Megan continued past her own exit and took the last one before the Delaware Water Gap. After a few miles, she downshifted and slipped from the deserted highway onto the dark, familiar county road. Now there were only headlights to see by and the glow from an occasional roadside tavern.

Jody stirred as the car paused at the crossroads that made up Deans Corner. He opened his eyes long enough to note the dark stores under the streetlights. A bank, grocery, grain and feed store and gas station were shut tight.

Megan turned right and the wide beam from her headlights bounced off the wrought-iron railing that separated the local cemetery from its fieldstone church. Beyond it, cultivated pastures stretched out over the hilltops and down along the sloping, rocky terrain, interrupted occasionally by the odd housing development or a cluster of dark farm buildings.

It was surrealistic under the artificial light. Much of the farmland was delineated by meandering stone drywall, dug and piled when the pastures were first cleared centuries earlier, as much to make the soil tillable as to keep anything in—or out. The car slowed down and Jody looked out to see sheep huddled on his right, their woolly faces caught in the high beams as they passed.

At the entrance of Valley View Farm, winter rye grew across the first stretch of level ground, waiting to be plowed under and planted in the first crop of cattle corn. Megan rounded one more gentle bend and slowed enough to ease the car from the hardtop of the county road onto the gravel driveway. The bumpy ride jostled Jody into full consciousness and the ruts beneath the wheels dissolved what was left of a Wall Street dream. He tried to stretch.

"Are we here?" he asked as he sat up and opened his eyes.

"Nearly."

He blinked and looked. Ahead of him through a sea of black, yellow light illuminated the front porch and a first-floor window of a large fieldstone house.

He looked at Megan's profile. "Where, exactly, is here?"

"Valley View, actually. I've brought you to the farm."

"Your family place?"

Megan turned to make sure he was fully awake and then stopped in the circular drive. "Yes. This is our house. I don't have an extra bedroom at my apartment and one of my father's sparc ones out here is certainly more comfortable than my couch." Even in the dim light, Jody could see her smile. She took the key from the ignition and the air was suddenly still.

"Considering the tenor of our conversation this evening, it's more appropriate, too."

She opened her door and let the cold night rush in. "It's not big on sophistication, but you'll get a good night's rest."

"Megan, it must be one in the morning. Aren't we disturbing your father?"

"I made arrangements." She got out of the car.

Jody opened his door and sort of rolled onto his feet, lifting his face to the still air. It smelled fresh, of spring earth. "Just out of curiosity, when did you have time to call home?"

"This isn't home any more."

"A minor point," he mumbled, though the fact that she'd brought it up said otherwise. They met at the trunk of the car. "Were these arrangements with your father made before or after you suggested it to me a few hours ago?"

"Before." She pulled out his suitcase and briefcase and slammed the trunk shut. "I like to cover my bases. I simply made sure that we could come out here if we needed to. As it turned out, we do."

"Why, Megan?"

She seemed startled by his near whisper. "Jody, I . . . you and I . . ."

"Feel something?" Before she could answer, he leaned forward and brushed his lips with his, pausing only long enough to savor the delicious ache it initiated.

"Jody!"

"I know. I'm breaking all the rules—half of which I made myself."

"You mustn't."

It was too dark to catch her expression as she quickly pivoted and approached the house. Even under the outside light, Megan turned away evasively. She was all business again, which was just as well. In his state, any response was a dangerous thing.

Neither of them talked and the only sound was their soft tread up the front steps and across the wide porch. At the front door Jody put his suitcase down while she fumbled with the key.

"My sleeping at Valley View wouldn't also have anything to do with Hugh O'Connor's sense of propriety where his daughters are concerned?"

Now she looked at him. "Don't be ridiculous. I needed a place to put you for the night, that's all."

He shrugged. "Your sister speaks very fondly of your father and his expectations."

"My father's liberal enough, not that it's relevant. Don't forget that Erin lived with your brother Matthew in Boston with Dad's full approval."

Jody leaned against the cool gray stone of the house. He was fully awake. "Erin *and* her college friend Nancy Reed lived with Matt. Matt considered himself a chaperon and he made that clear to your father, as clear as Hugh O'Connor's expectations were to Matt."

"A lot of good it did. Erin still fell in love with his oldest brother." She stopped and looked hard at the doorknob. "I'm sorry, I shouldn't have said that. I'm tired. Let's go in."

Jody crossed his arms. "I know you've tried to talk her out of it."

"As I've said, Erin doesn't need my approval—or anybody's. Stop questioning me. I feel like I'm on the witness stand."

"You could plead the Fifth Amendment."

"Discussing Erin and Kevin will hardly incriminate me. You already know how I feel."

"You think your sister jumped the track. There she was at a Harvard teaching hospital right in Boston—can't do better than that. She was living in Back Bay with the world at her feet. Along comes some brawling cranberry grower, with dirt under his fingernails, his heart in the sand hills, and poor innocent Erin is swept away. Down the tubes she goes and gives it all up for love, fool that she is."

Megan opened the door and looked at him with defiance. "You've being melodramatic and I'm too tired for conversation, personal or otherwise. Erin lives her life and I live mine."

"But you lost your role model."

The front hall was dim, illuminated only by the single lamp left on in the living room. "Jody, what I've lost or gained is none of your business. I brought you out here to discuss conservation and protection of groundwater supplies, which we'll do tomorrow. Now stop sounding like a lawyer and follow me up to bed."

"That sounds remarkably appealing." He laughed and she scowled.

"I liked you better asleep." Megan led the way up the staircase. With no more than a casual, "I'll see you in the morning, sleep as long as you like," she opened a bedroom door and snapped on a light.

"Where's your father's room?"

"Between yours and mine."

"Can't trust yourself?"

Instead of the expected glare, she cocked her head and considered it. "Wishful thinking, Counselor," she replied and pointed across the hall to a darkened threshold. "The bathroom's over there. I'll use it first and be out of your way." She left him, crossed the landing and closed the bathroom door behind her.

Megan O'Connor was an appealing woman. It had been a long time since Jody had let anyone, male or female, talk him into rescheduling an entire weekend and he'd done it as much for his own curiosity as for Megan's earthshaking public service project.

In the dark, Jody lay in bed with his arms folded beneath his head and looked at the ceiling. Denials aside, she came very close to his ideal: intelligent and motivated but independent, damned attractive and not—by any stretch of the imagination—interested in what David Howell would call entanglements.

Under normal circumstances, with all that had gone on between them in the course of the evening, Jody would have expected to find himself in far different quarters than a spare bedroom with a father on the other side of the wall. The fantasy of what might have transpired stirred him until he had to shift position.

He reminded himself of the circumstances. This was networking at its most intimate. He and this blue-eyed business associate were also bound by the threads that wove family together, threads that could come back to tie you in knots.

There was also the small fact that Megan O'Connor wasn't interested in him—not, apparently, on any level. Again, Jody thought of David Howell. Megan's goals were carved in stone and whether she would admit to it or not, her disapproval of her sister Erin's "jumping the track" was palpable.

There was a younger O'Connor sister, too. Bridget was a senior in a New Hampshire college. Maybe the goals, the determination and the role modeling were for her benefit, as well. Hugh O'Connor was a widower, which meant his daughters had only each other to rely on for direction and support. Maybe that had something to do with the source of Megan's disappointment. Jody was just stubborn enough to consider finding out and just tired enough to put it aside and fall asleep.

Saturday morning Jody awoke to sunshine. He'd brought comfortable clothes to New York and now he pulled on old burgundy corduroys and a flannel shirt. The house was quiet, except for the floorboards creaking beneath his feet, and he found Hugh O'Connor in the kitchen.

"Always delighted to have another Branigan under my roof, if only for the weekend," he said heartily as he shook Jody's hand. "Megan's gone to Hackettstown to see about the interview. I suppose she's told you she thinks the station's going to be sold. Rumor has it they'll bring in their own from Chicago and she'll be transferred."

"Transferred? She gave me the impression the interview was to save her job here."

"Wishful thinking or outright misinformation. Your neck of the woods doesn't suit her grand ideas. The affiliate's in Plymouth." He laughed at Jody's astonishment. "The idea doesn't sit well, but she's come up empty in this area. She's putting your interview together as a demo, to give the station manager an idea of her skill. She's good. They'll see that."

"A demo."

"Suits me fine, having her up there with her sister. She hasn't mentioned any of this to Erin, yet, but I think she should share Erin's place till the wedding, then have that little carriage house to herself. She's got dreams of some Park Avenue penthouse, of course.''

Share that little carriage house! Millbrook! ''I can see that,'' Jody replied.

Hugh waved at the air. ''Someday, fine. But right now, while she gets her bearings, I like the idea of her being looked after.''

''Looked after?''

''She's out of the nest, but knowing there are six Branigans around does a father's heart good.''

Jody swallowed. ''And what about Valley View? Are you banking on any of your daughters coming back?''

Hugh shook his head. ''It's a partnership with my brother, Rob. His side of the family'll keep it going.'' He made breakfast and talked of Kevin's visit the previous Christmas and his delight at the upcoming wedding. He was a strapping Irish-American who'd found a kindred spirit in his future son-in-law.

Together they walked out to the barn where Jody met Robert O'Connor and insisted on a tour of the dairy operation. The herd of Holsteins were out to pasture and the spring air was ripe with the musk of the farm. Reluctantly, the tour ended, Jody left Hugh at the barn and went back to the house in order to work.

The day was blustery, with bright sun and a biting breeze. Fruit trees were flowering, daffodils covered the south side of the lawn and violets offered a mat of color along the winding entrance.

Away from the barn, the air smelled faintly of woodsmoke. The stove in the kitchen as well as the fireplace in the den were going. It was at Hugh's desk in the den that Jody laid out the Branigan file he needed to study. With a cup of coffee, he lost himself in work for his brothers, this time an application to revitalize nonproductive bogs to expand Bittersweet production.

An hour later he got up to tend the fire and the sound of Megan's "Good morning" had him turning toward the doorway.

Megan, too, had traded her suit for country attire. She was in trousers and a teal-blue sweater that accentuated her figure and added fathoms to her eyes. They sparkled and her hair shone. The moment she entered the room, Jody caught the drift of the same perfume. In the daylight she was riveting.

She looked confident about turning Jody's memory lapse into her personal success. Fate had dealt her a perfect hand and it was up to her to sort out the cards.

"You look triumphant," Jody said to the embers.

"We're all set to record at the studio. I've put together a new set of questions." She stopped next to him. "I want to make clear how much I appreciate this, Jody. You know how cutthroat the communications business is. I do feel a little guilty about driving you out here and disrupting your weekend. I need you or I wouldn't have insisted."

"Insisted, coaxed, cajoled and dragged and all I was hoping for was seduced."

She laughed softly. "I know you're teasing, but I do apologize."

Jody considered her smile. She didn't look the least bit apologetic. "I'm no stranger to hard work and perseverance but maybe you owe your thanks to a fortuitous set of unforeseen circumstances."

"The fact that you forgot my interview?"

"Yes."

She smiled but offered nothing more. How long would it be until she admitted to the whole story?

Five

———

He finished tending the fire and dusted his hands.

"Sleep well?" she asked.

"Yes, thanks. Ate well, too, and Hugh introduced me to some Holsteins. Impressive operation."

"Have you spent much time with Dad?"

"We had quite a conversation over breakfast." He watched her and caught a glimmer of something. Doubt? "He's proud of you."

"He taught me the value of hard work."

"And the need to be flexible when things don't always turn out the way you'd planned?"

"What?"

"Apparently there's a chance you'll soon be sharing your sister's carriage house."

"You know." She turned away from him.

Jody touched her and kept his hand on her sleeve until she looked back at him. "Couldn't you have told me last night?"

"Erin doesn't even know and it hasn't happened yet. I'm holding out for a miracle, otherwise she and Kevin will laugh themselves silly. I've made such a scene about Millbrook and the bogs and all of you.... It's humiliating."

"You could have trusted me."

Megan looked at him for a long moment. "You're different, I know, but underneath blood's thicker than water, especially Branigan blood."

His Branigan blood was warming, and for his own good, he let go of her arm.

Megan cleared her throat. "I apologize. I hope that makes you feel better. There's no need to involve you in my problems. We'll get down to business this afternoon. You're here for the interview, Jody. I have a lot to learn from you."

"Yes, you do," he said.

She held his glance with a sharp look of her own and then stirred a log. "I'm glad to see you brought some comfortable clothes," she said at last.

"After-hours, I like a change, even in a hotel room."

She looked at her father's desk, now strewn with Jody's papers. "I thought you might have stayed outside. It's a nice day."

He shook his head. "Family business. If I can't work in Plymouth this weekend, then I have to work here. I need some time alone though. I'll be finished in a while."

"Excuse me, I didn't know you weren't to be disturbed."

"Megan, everything about you disturbs me."

"It shouldn't."

"When has that ever made any difference?"

She didn't answer. Instead she went back to the doorway. "The taping's at two o'clock. I'll need you by twelve-thirty or one. I hope that suits."

"You're in the driver's seat. Guess it'll have to." Again she looked disconcerted by his tone.

"Go back to work. I'm sorry if I disturbed you."

Jody looked at those blue, unreadable eyes and closed his own. Yes, she most certainly did.

Megan, all business, returned to the den with lunch on a tray and gave him time to eat. She reviewed what she would ask as they drove to the radio station. Again she explained that now with David Howell in the local picture, Jody was to discuss wetlands protection in general and then cite Massachusetts's Plymouth County examples.

The taping went well. Once in front of the microphone, Megan led him through a layman's discussion of the problems rural areas faced with encroaching development. Jody responded by citing federal statutes and then, on cue, homed in on his own territory. This was easy enough to do as the Branigan Cranberries bog operation bordered on conservation land. As the company's attorney, Jody made sure his brothers followed the Clean Water Act to the letter. He was concise, professional and easy to understand.

The understated sensuality so evident when Megan spoke transposed itself for the microphone. Her professional voice was well modulated, soft, with crisp enunciation. Still, it registered in Jody the way it had the night before. It was a pleasure to listen to her.

At three-fifteen Megan called it a wrap and waved a thank-you to the technician in the control room. She was glowing. "That gives me more than enough air time, with room to edit. Thanks, Jody, you were right on target."

"I hope it helps." He laughed.

"Yes?"

"You're doing your best to convince a station manager to transfer you to a place you hate."

"One of life's little ironies," she said sarcastically.

He shrugged. "Once you're in Millbrook you'll be closer to Erin. You can convince her in person to call off the engagement."

"Don't think it hasn't occurred to me."

"You wouldn't be the first, not for any of the Branigan women." His term was deliberate. Jody slid his chair back and ignored her surprise. "I'm a free man at last?"

"Yes, I guess you are."

"Will you work on the tape this afternoon?"

"No, Monday's soon enough. I won't cut anything until I've added what I can get from David."

"And will you treat him to a weekend with the cows?"

They were on their way to the parking lot and Megan shot him a pained look. "No cows for David."

"He's more the Maison Provence type."

"I really don't know what type he is, Jody."

"Do you bring many men home?"

Megan turned. "You're not the first, but no, my father and I rarely agree on the men in my life."

"He doesn't go for the upwardly mobile type?"

She smiled a little woodenly. "Haven't you noticed that the less personal we are, the better we get along?"

"Are you changing the subject?"

"Yes. Do you listen to WJQG?"

He let the subject drop and followed her line of discussion. "Sure, it's just outside Plymouth. It covers most of the south shore."

"Good. This may be a demo, but I was telling the truth about getting it on the air. When I've lined all that up, I'll let you know when it's scheduled."

"It is as easy as that?"

"No, but I'm in public relations. Convincing people is part of my job, part of what I do best."

"I'll have to agree."

They were quiet, each getting their bearing. Finally, as Megan reached the car, she looked over the hood at him. "Do you regret staying over? Has it been so bad?"

"Pleasant mostly, and informative."

"You look a little more rested. You could use a week out here."

They got in and when he'd sat down, he put his head back. "I could use a week just about anywhere."

"That bad?" The engine turned over and Megan began the return trip to Valley View.

"Not bad, I just don't have your enthusiasm anymore."

"I get a little carried away. I'm independent and I'm aggressive, but I have to be. In this business, you have to make noise to get noticed."

"You'll be noticed, Megan."

"Thank you, Jody. That means a lot. Compliments don't come easily from you, do they?"

"I'm not a flatterer." Having touched on something personal made him quiet again.

Megan turned to look at him as she drove. "You've had a great time digging at me. What's got you so strung out?"

"Nothing more than the usual."

"Want to talk about it?" There it was again, the unexpected dip in her voice, half an octave. His heart raced, and he revelled in the ways Megan reminded him that he was alive and that he was male.

However he replied, "No point," and he meant it.

"Touché," she said softly.

They returned to Valley View in fairly comfortable silence, broken by occasional conversation and the strains from the radio. Megan stopped at the Allamuchy overlook and Jody admired the view. After a week in Manhattan, his body ached for fresh air while his psyche longed for a simple pleasure, not connected with legal briefs, shop talk or pending litigation. Any of a number of pleasures might do.

"Is it safe to assume you're finished with me?" he asked as they got back in the car.

"Yes, and I do appreciate everything, really. I know I've put you through a lot."

"Any chance we could make the airport this evening?"

Megan looked genuinely surprised. "Yes, I guess so. I thought you'd stay over tonight and we'd get you to the airport in the morning."

"Doesn't seem much point."

She drove in silence for a moment. "Dad'll be disappointed. I know he was looking forward to spending some time with you. Who's waiting in Plymouth?"

Jody closed his eyes, tempted to make up something outrageous. Instead he was truthful. "'My mistress, the sea,' " he quoted. "A walk on a deserted beach. A beer at the marina while I look at my boat."

She was smiling. "Sounds lovely. Your Sunday rituals?"

"Yes, I suppose so. It clears my head, helps me face Monday."

"Are Mondays that bad?"

"They can be." He watched the countryside slide past as they left the interstate and meandered through Deans Corner. "It's pretty out here. You could work in New York and still be close to this. But I suppose success for you means getting away from here and heading for the Big Apple."

She pulled up in front of the house. "Yes, I guess it does."

Once again they climbed the front steps and walked across the porch. There was a swing, suspended from chains, at the edge. "A nice touch," he said. "I didn't notice it last night."

"A bit old-fashioned for my taste." She stood still. "Shall I drive you to Newark?"

Jody hesitated, glancing at the vistas behind her. The late afternoon sun was still bright. Down the slope, beyond the narcissi, the immense barn with its silos waited for the herd to return from their hillside pasture. The air smelled of woodsmoke and fresh dirt, as distinctive as the mud-flats and tidal pools of Plymouth. "Megan, what do you want me to do?"

"Me? I think I've asked enough of you, Jody. You call the shots, do what you like. If there's nobody waiting at home, don't rush off. Frankly, I think you could use the rest. Stay here, relax, unwind. Dad would enjoy dinner with you."

"And you?"

She looked uncomfortable. "I have a previous engagement, as they say."

"A date."

"Yes. I'll be going back to my place. But that doesn't mean you shouldn't stay. It might do you some good to relax. I'll be back for you first thing in the morning."

"Break your date, Megan."

"Jody, I can't do that! It's four o'clock already."

"I'm not asking any more of you than you expected of me."

"Is this some kind of silly test? Retribution?"

Maybe it was. Jody couldn't have answered truthfully. He didn't know. "You rearranged my entire weekend. I'm asking for the same courtesy."

"It isn't necessary. You and my father—" She stopped. "You're doing this on purpose."

Jody put his hands in his pockets and glanced out at the view again. "Think whatever you want. I stay if you stay."

"This isn't a game!"

He smiled at her. "Take it or leave it."

Megan looked out over the fields. "What makes you think I'll be pleasant company?"

"It hasn't been altogether unpleasant so far." The wind caught his hair. "Go make your phone call. There's no deserted beach, but there's lots of wide open space out there. Nice time of day for a walk. I'll be along that ridge."

"Just like that?"

"Just like that."

Their conversation was peppered with pauses, obviously awkward for somebody as surefooted as Megan. "Jody, I don't know what's behind those green eyes of yours, but you're apt to be very disappointed. What are you expecting?''

''Your company. I'm banking on the fact that for a few hours, you can make me forget the work in my briefcase and on Hugh O'Connor's desk.'' Without giving her time to reply, he turned for the pasture.

He left Megan on the porch and followed a well-worn path through a break in the low stone wall, up along the crest of a hill. His light tone and teasing words belied the pressure he was feeling. He started his walk deep in thought about the pending Branigan proposition.

He crossed the crest of the hill and reached a stand of pines, so absorbed in his thoughts he hadn't seen a thing. Angrily he swore at his preoccupation, then turned to retrace his steps. Megan was coming through the opening in the wall behind him.

Jody stood and watched her. The sun was low and the light made her hair shine. She waved to catch his attention, then jogged slowly in his direction. Her unconscious grace cleared his head and he stood, waiting for her.

She moved over the rocky path with a steady gait and he wondered how often she'd climbed this trail as a child. How many times had she and her sisters come out here and shared secrets and dreams the way he'd walked the bogs and talked with Ryan and Matt?

Her physical appeal intensified as she approached him. Gently panting and slightly embarrassed, she brushed her hair from her face. Given any encouragement, he would have pulled her into his arms.

''You win,'' she said when she'd reached him.

''In the battle of wills?''

"I've been rude, Jody. I apologize. The date's postponed."

"Was it someone you're serious about?"

She shook her head.

"Are you serious about anyone?"

She paused. "No."

"Good. Then give me a tour and keep my mind off my work," he replied.

"The view should do that." So much for encouragement. "Still thinking about all that stuff in the den?"

He nodded and they walked a bit without talking.

Finally, Megan broke the silence. "Tell me about your boat. All Erin's told me about are the cranberry bogs. Is it motor or sail?"

"Sail. Matt and I own an eighteen-foot catboat, fairly common up there. It's big and wide, pretty under sail. Gaff rigged, like the old working skiffs they're based on."

"Do you cruise?"

"When I can. Matt finishes medical school in June and we'll take it out before he starts his internship. I don't have much time to get away, either, but it's nice to know it's there."

"A luxury you can afford."

"Yes, I guess I can."

"When will you put it in the water?"

"Soon. You might think about taking a sail when you're in Millbrook for the wedding, or any other time if the job pans out."

"I'd like that."

"A sail or to wind up in Millbrook?"

Megan looked out at the rolling hills. "We were talking about the boat. Until it's launched, you visit the boatyard and check her out on Sunday afternoons?"

"Keeps me sane. The boat and the bogs."

"Erin told me you still work with your brothers. How on earth do you find the time?"

The honey in her voice was better than a tranquilizer. "I make time. My mental health depends on it and the exercise doesn't do me any harm, either."

"You're in great shape," she mused and then laughed. "I apologize for barging in on you yesterday afternoon. That was quite an introduction."

He envisioned it and let the memory dance. "I'll take that as a compliment."

"I should apologize for what I've said about Kevin. I was too blunt last night."

"You're entitled to your opinions, Megan."

"Thank you. I have nothing against your family, Jody."

"It's just not the right one for Erin to be marrying into," he replied.

"Marriage is forever. Kevin's the first man she's ever been involved with. There's no basis for comparison."

"In bed?"

"That's not what I meant." She wasn't flustered but her eyes were bright.

"But it could be just sex?"

"You Branigans are very physically appealing. Certainly Erin might be all caught up in that. I know her the way you know your brothers. She'll need more, in time. Kevin's had his own life, gone his own way for years. I'm sure he's talked her into things, persuaded her. He's more than ten years older than she is. You have to admit, she's risking everything by marrying him.''

Jody watched the animation in her face and listened to concern that said as much about Megan as the sister she was worried about. "There's risk in anything that's worthwhile. You think it's possible that my brother proposed just to make an honest woman out of Erin. Maybe to keep your father happy?"

"I know you're teasing, but it's very possible. Erin and Kevin were leading such different lives, Kevin might have thought she'd never accept."

"To your way of thinking, Kevin's stuck and Erin's making a huge mistake. Instead she should have bedded down till she got my brother out of her system, then gone back to her life in Boston."

His honesty put color in her cheeks. "Crudely put, Jody."

"Nevertheless, that's what you would have done, I assume."

Megan looked down the slope at the sheep eating their feed. "I would have used my head."

"Then you've never been in love. Erin leads with her heart. You're a lot more pragmatic than your sister."

"Pragmatism wouldn't hurt! She's not the affair type, so instead she's changed jobs, moved into some carriage house in the middle of nowhere and set a wedding date."

Jody was quiet, caught between the urge to argue and defend and the urge to involve himself in Megan's line of reasoning.

She was looking at him. "You think I've been too blunt but for Erin's sake someone has to be."

"Things could be worse. She could have given up everything and moved right in with Kevin. At least she's given herself some breathing room."

"I hardly think they're sleeping in separate beds." Concern played in her features and she sighed. "I didn't mean to be insulting last night. It's just that I worry about her. Erin's too innocent for your Branigan brand of charm."

Jody let a flip reply pass. "We all worried."

"Wonderful! Is that supposed to cheer me up?"

Megan looked stricken and Jody touched her. "Kevin most of all." He waited for her to turn and look at him and then he leaned back against the wall. "Kevin didn't do anything to pursue her. In fact, he wanted me to date her. He wanted her to stay in Boston with Matt. Kevin never told any of us what was going on because, at first, I'm not sure he could make sense of it himself."

"Given time these things run their course, Jody."

The air was full of starlings, a black flock that shifted with the breeze was settled in the empty cornfield. While they landed Jody gathered his thoughts and measured his words. "You're very different from Erin, as different as I am from Kevin. You can't judge what they mean to each other by your experience with men. *Affairs* run their course, Megan. They were meant to because they only fill some temporary need. Erin and Kevin are two sides of the same coin."

"For the moment. What if a few years from now Erin sees what she's done, realizes how much she's given up?"

"Maybe she already sees what she's gained."

"You're an arrogant bunch," Megan replied lightly.

"It's helped us survive. Survival's something we're very good at. Everything I am, all the years of tuition, law school, all came from Kevin's determination. Sometimes that did take arrogance. He had to stop being a teenager and start being an adult the day our parents died. For Kevin there was never time to just lie back and grow up. It happened overnight and overnight he took on responsibility for five other lives. He was seventeen years old."

"And how can someone with that much authority, someone who has been the boss all those years, ever give Erin her own space, let alone equal time? Don't you see how she'll be smothered?"

"Your sister would never let anyone smother her! She has her career at the Women's Clinic in Millbrook. She's lived her own life and now she wants to wrap it around Kevin's. Don't look so doubtful. Your sister's made him believe that there's somebody there for him, finally. She makes him laugh and she's the only woman I know who's been able to tease that arrogance out of him.

"Megan, she makes him dream. His only dreams were for his brothers. Your sister didn't want Matt or me, she wanted Kevin, and if he has anything to say about it, she'll never be sorry." The heat of his words lingered between them.

"I hope not," Megan murmured finally. "Forever's a long time."

"Scares the hell out of you, doesn't it?"

"No, Jody, it's just that I'm far more interested in tomorrow than I am in forever."

Six

_____

Jody picked clover from the field. "Since last night, I've resolved half a dozen times not to get embroiled in family matters with you. You've got your life all wrapped up in a nice neat package. The Plymouth station may be a detour, but there's no doubt in my mind that you'll even work that to your advantage. Communications, broadcasting, a suburban station, then the jump to New York and Saturday night dates in Manhattan. That's fine, Megan. I wish you well. But it doesn't suit everybody."

"It suited Erin fine. She had the same goals and the same dreams."

"And you can't stand the fact that she altered them? Life doesn't always go according to plan. From Kevin right down to Matthew, any Branigan will tell you it's a damned dangerous way to live."

"Any and all Branigans."

"We like giving advice."

Megan shook her head. "Can't you see the influence your brother has had? Erin didn't alter her dreams, Kevin did it for her."

"You greatly underestimate your sister and if you believe that, you don't know her half as well as I do."

"In your family, I can't imagine that a woman stands a chance on her own."

Distance! Jody turned on his heels and began to walk, taking long, purposeful strides. Megan managed to trot until she caught up.

"Jody—"

He waved away the comment. "This is pointless. In my family, no one has to be on his or her own. No one wants to be."

Megan turned away from him and Jody took her by the shoulders. The softness of the wool under his fingers surprised him as much as the startled expression in her wide eyes. "No one stands a chance with any of you," she whispered.

She shook off his hands and walked halfway down the slope where she sat among the rocks of the sheep pasture. Jody stood where she'd left him and damned his family, damned hers, railed against the complications and then followed. He sat next to her and neither spoke. The silence, however, grew comfortable in a way that stymied his legal mind and soothed his soul.

"This was our favorite picnic spot, Bridget's, Erin's and mine. You could watch the sheep on one side and the cows on the other. My mother used to knit from our wool. 'Pick a sheep,' she'd say. 'That'll be your sweater for fall.'"

Jody relaxed. "Has it been hard without her?"

"Not as tough as it must have been for you. We were nearly grown up when we lost her and we still had my father, not to mention my aunt who lives over the hill."

"I guess you can't blame Hugh for being protective," Jody said. "Three daughters to keep on the straight and narrow."

"No harder than if we'd been three sons," she replied defensively.

"Were you a handful?"

"Me?" Megan turned and looked at him. Her expression was wide open, curious and still full of concern.

"You still are," he replied. "Live your own life, Megan. Make your own mistakes and let Erin make hers."

"Life is less painful if the mistakes can be avoided in the first place."

"Kevin loves her, Megan, as much as he's loved any of us." It came from his heart and the intimacy, in contrast to her quip, made them both stop. "Erin knows it."

Tears welled from the corners of her eyes and disappeared under a quick blink. Melt her heart! Their shoulders rubbed and he looked at the pattern of the yoke of her sweater. "Did your mother knit this?"

"Yes."

Lightly, he traced the ribbing and concentrated on the feel of the wool under his fingers. "Matches your eyes," he murmured. His heartbeat quickened as he moved his hand over the fine work, but he stopped at the swell of her breast.

"You're going to kiss me, aren't you?" she whispered.

"Yes."

"Don't complicate things, Jody," she added.

"I can't think of anything simpler."

She laughed softly and he felt it on his cheek. Encouraged, he tilted her face with his hand. With the exception of Megan O'Connor's presence, it had been a long time since his body had responded to anything but work or fatigue. Desire compelled him and anticipation made his heart hammer.

He felt her hand against the back of his head and her fingers in his hair. The sensation had his scalp tingling in such marked contrast to his usual tension headaches that he sighed as he smiled at her.

Her touch seeped slowly through his shoulders, into his chest, and he closed his eyes. Her mouth was soft, yielding, far warmer than the air and he kissed her without any urgency, savoring her reaction as she shifted against him. The small pleasures intensified where she touched him. Against the pliancy of her breasts he felt the steady pounding of his own heart, a sounding board, sure and true, waking everything he held at bay.

How did she do that? How could she suspend the urgency of his real life and dissolve all pressures when the very fact of who she was should have deepened them? On the hill in the last of the spring afternoon, kissing her filled him with pleasure. He welcomed the desire that seized him.

He felt the softness of her cheek under his thumb and the gentle exploration of her tongue against his, tantalizing in its hesitation, no more than a tentative step beyond the chaste kiss of the night before, yet brimming with promise.

"Jody," she moaned, full of caution.

It was appropriate; somebody had to put on the brakes. When he brushed the fullness of her breast, she moved his hand.

He nuzzled her neck. "I'm complicating things?"

"You could be."

"If I had a little encouragement?"

She looked downright wicked. "Shall I start with a button on your shirt or go right for the belt buckle?"

His breath caught behind his breastbone as his blood rushed to meet her suggested destinations.

Megan shifted away from him. "Right this minute, if I headed for the bedroom, you'd follow like a sailor on shore leave." In a sudden movement, she put her arms around his neck, kissed him and pulled back. "I know what's going on with this perfect body of yours. What I'm after is the stuff behind those gorgeous green eyes."

How did she do that, leave him weak-kneed and bawled out in the same breath?

"Haven't we talked?"

She held up her hand. "Yes, indeed, about me, about my erroneous impressions of your family, about my philosophy of life, my goals. You've managed to keep me on the defensive since last night."

As if fighting hiccups, Jody concentrated on his erratic breathing. "You need some straightening out."

"I'm entitled to my opinions!"

"Not when they're wrong! I've been defending my brothers all my life, mostly to strangers. You're not a stranger, Megan. I don't want you in their camp," he blurted.

He stopped and looked into her eyes and after a moment, her lips parted. "I'm flattered that you care, but why? Why does it matter so much?"

Why! He couldn't bring himself to consider any more than the familial connection. "Because of Erin. I care about her and I care about Kevin. They won't be completely happy until you see their relationship for what it is."

"So you've extended your weekend to stay and argue their case?"

"I'm here at your invitation."

Her laugh was self-deprecating. "I asked for that one."

"I don't sense much regret on your part."

She arched her eyebrows. "No, but I haven't asked to be kissed senseless every time my guard's down."

"Kissing you has been the only bright spot in a hellish week. I'm apt to do it again."

She laughed and he loved it. "You argue one minute and flatter the next. Do you know what you want from me?"

He balled his fists against their tingling. "To set you straight about the family. What you see for us is a long line of casual affairs."

"And your behavior is supposed to change my mind?"

He felt the hated, inevitable heat sweep across the bridge of his nose and over his cheekbones.

Megan had the audacity to sit and follow the course with her wide, amused glance. "Go on, Jody."

"Affairs, punctuated by an occasional marriage of the barefoot and pregnant variety. You're underestimating the women and that includes your sister."

She stiffened.

"We've been in a fishbowl for twenty years. You have to understand that the way things were, the way we grew up, has put all of us on the defensive. Concern, if not disapproval, has come hand in glove with every serious romance my brothers have had. I've watched it all, since I was a kid. Branigans were too young, too old, too wild, too middle class."

"I'm sorry."

"People thought Kevin carried too much responsibility or Ryan wouldn't accept any. Drew was too headstrong and Sean was too angry. Matt hasn't even taken the time to test the waters and I can't blame him. Too different was what it always boiled down to, that houseful of boys and that bachelor up the hill. We built a bulwark against the world for some very good reasons. Can you find fault with that?"

"No."

"It's made us all gun-shy, but it also brought extraordinary women into my brothers' lives. They have to be. Megan, your worries are nothing new. Kevin deserves a life of his own and he's found it with someone strong and vital enough to convince him of it."

The moment he finished, he regretted most of what he'd said and all of what it had revealed. Silently he blamed his high color on the wind. Jody got up, shoved his hands into his pockets and set out across the ridge. The ground was rocky, bare in spots and green in others. He kept his glance on the view, focusing on the church steeple and the back of the feed store in the distance.

At first he thought she had returned to the house, but Megan finally caught up. They looked at each other again and fell into a tentative silence, punctuated only by the call of crows and the whine of a car on an unseen road. She picked up a stone and looked up at Jody. "Thank you."

He shrugged. "I love my brother and I love your sister for what she's given him."

"And you, Jody, what about you?"

Seven

He should have seen it coming. "What about me?"

"Too wild? Too angry for some woman to tame? Too perfect?"

"Too busy."

Megan leaned over and pulled his hand from his pocket, then tugged until he joined her on the ground. "I'm beginning to believe that."

His heart thumped. "Megan O'Connor, you'll believe what you want."

"And if I want to believe your busyness is a smoke screen?"

"You'd be foolish."

"You're pushing thirty, Mr. Perfect. There must have been one or two serious relationships along the way."

"Nothing I couldn't say goodbye to."

"Interesting choice of words."

"Anything beyond casual takes time and energy. I'm short on both."

"You're hedging."

"You're prying," he said.

"You just told me that a lot of what you are is a product of Kevin's dreams and values, even his ambition. I can't pry into his life so I'm prying into yours. For the sake of my sister, you understand."

"What other reason could there be?"

"None."

He wanted her expression to say otherwise, but she suggested dinner, stood up and started for the house. He left her at the crest of the hill and headed for the barn, found the male O'Connors and let them put him to work. Forty-five minutes later, when he and Hugh returned to the house, Megan had the meal started. She'd taken off her sweater and pulled a chef's apron over her white cotton turtleneck. Jody thought better of telling her how happily domestic she looked.

She wrinkled her nose, but with affection. "You've both got time to get rid of the cows. Go and shower. Dad, the steak's all yours, and, Jody, I'm leaving the salad up to you."

They had a simple but delicious meal in the dining room and dessert in front of the newly rekindled fire. Conversation touched on environmental law, the summer wedding and the Branigans, then the O'Connors, the farm and the communications business.

Jody talked of Millbrook and the career possibilities in Boston, were Megan to land at WJQG, as she feared. Hugh said good-night early and left them to the dying fire. Jody stood up as his host left the room, then settled back on the couch next to Megan. She was looking at the desk.

"Tell me about the work over there."

"Just family business."

"Cranberries?"

"Yes."

"Wetlands protection?"

"Some."

"Jody Branigan, do I have to get up and go read those papers myself?"

He laughed. "Dry stuff. You wouldn't be interested."

Her eyes were clear and bright. "Counselor, last night I talked about wetlands with you and your associates. This afternoon we spent hours discussing legal issues for the interview. How can you say I wouldn't be interested?"

He was lost in her gaze, enchanted by the thickness of the lashes fringing her eyelids. "Until twenty-four hours ago the idea of growing cranberries for a living was abhorrent."

She touched his arm and shook her head slowly. Her hair swung gracefully along the line of her jaw. "Never abhorrent. That's like saying I can't stand dairy farming."

"Just not suitable for the O'Connor women."

"We're getting off the subject, Jody. I asked because I'm interested in what's taking up all your time."

She emphasized "your" and his circulatory system kicked into high gear. "My free time—if you can call it that—is taken up at the moment with what we're calling the Taft Proposal. Drew and Holly want to expand Bittersweet Bogs. They've bought a parcel of land from the Taft family that includes bogs no longer in operation. Holly and my brothers want to bring the bogs back into operation and establish a few more."

"Sounds simple enough."

"In principle, it is. However, the operation is considered lapsed because it's been out of production three of the past five years. The amount of paperwork is massive. Permits must be filed on the local, state and federal levels. The EPA, conservation commissions and Department of Environmental Quality Engineering—DEQE—all get involved."

"Exhausting and frustrating?"

He nodded. "Yes, but I like the challenge."

"Even though you barely have time for anything else?"

"It keeps me in touch with my family."

"At long last?" she asked.

His eyebrows knit into a question mark.

Megan laughed. "Erin's told me all about 'Kevin's brilliant younger brothers.' I gather the older ones have pushed to make sure you'd succeed, kept you away from the bogs so you could concentrate on getting through school, made sure you didn't have to worry about all the nitty-gritty goings-on in Millbrook."

"Perceptive."

"Does that bother you?"

Did it? "I don't know, Megan. Maybe. I'm not one for analysis. My family assumed the way they handled things for me was the right thing to do. I'll admit, it made life easier for me."

"Until now when you're working double time. No wonder you're so strung out."

"Am I?"

"You don't need to hear it from me." There it was again, the husky, half-octave drop in her voice, mesmerizing in its soothing sensuality. Megan leaned back against the sofa cushions and the intimacy of the conversation settled into him.

How long had it been since he'd talked about himself, since he'd let anyone speculate on the impetus behind his actions? He needed to hear it from her. He was curious, infatuated, puzzled by the depth of his reaction to Megan and her questions.

As if others had come into the room, Megan kept her voice low. "What's your ultimate goal, Jody, making partner in your firm? Running for office? Kevin thinks you're destined for politics and that you'd make a great governor."

Kevin thinks. "Kevin's not infallible."

Megan raised her eyebrows. "The cranberry baron's human, after all?"

Jody closed his eyes and leaned back. Their shoulders touched. "My relationship with my brother has nothing to do with his love for Erin, the rightness of it."

"If you criticize him, are you afraid I might, too?"

"I'd like to change the subject."

"Too personal? Not for the man who kissed me breathless out in the pasture this afternoon and lectured me the whole time on the perfection of life in Millbrook, as Branigans lead it. You've got me under a microscope. I'm entitled to a little speculating."

His attempt to keep her at bay was halfhearted. He was relaxed in a way he'd forgotten existed, a way that kept his pulse quick and his wits sharp. "You might be disappointed."

"Perhaps. Then again, Counselor, I might be pleasantly surprised."

"I have been," he heard himself say, and her soft laugh blanketed him.

"Thank you. You're much more than I expected. Much more complicated, actually, probably because you're holding back so much."

He considered what she'd said, but didn't answer.

"Is it tough, living up to all those great expectations?" Megan added.

His answer came slowly and he closed his eyes. "Yes."

Eight

Megan's fingers splayed over his chest. Her touch was light and beneath her hand his heart pounded savagely. He kept his eyes closed and savored the recurrent surprise that the source of his pleasure was Megan O'Connor.

"The Taft project is a way to pay them back?" she was saying.

"At first, I guess all the legal help was."

"But now?"

Lest she pull her hand away, he didn't move; he just opened his eyes and feasted on her nearness. "Now it's more of a bridge. A lifeline."

He listened to his own words. All night it had been as if someone else were speaking for him, a swimmer coming up from a dark sea, getting closer and closer to the surface. Discontent, restlessness, frustration had been brewing for months, but never had he put it into words, even to himself.

A lifeline? A bridge! Back to the bogs? Before the conversation degenerated into a full-blown confession, he leaned forward and touched her face.

Her expression had changed while he'd had his eyes closed. Megan was soft, sensuous in a way that matched her voice. Her hand still rested on his chest, but she pressed her palm harder, as if to contain the hammering in it.

The remedy to all confession, family analysis and soul searching was inches from him. Megan parted her lips, and conversation died. He didn't kiss her. Instead, he raised his own hand and slowly placed it exactly as she had hers. He pressed gently over the fullness of her breast. His fingers curved upward over the softness, and the heel of his thumb rested against her ribs. "Thunder," he whispered.

"You, too."

The den of Valley View Farm...Hugh O'Connor asleep above them...family...fishbowl...all of it would keep things in control. The brakes had to stay on.

As he leaned closer, Megan tilted her chin and arched her back. Beneath the single layer of her cotton jersey and the sheer fabric of her bra, he felt her strain against him. With his thumb, he explored the hardening bud of her nipple.

"Jody," she gasped. "I don't understand any of this. It doesn't make sense."

"I know." Desire danced, teased, tore at him. She explored his chest with her thumb and then traced the rough stubble of his jaw. She played with the buttons of his shirt and when he put his free arm around her back, she clung to him until they lay together in the soft contours of the couch.

He kissed her. Megan was beneath him, against him, fully dressed yet molded perfectly into the crook of his shoulder, the curve of his hip. He didn't dare tug the jersey from her slacks. Keeping fabric between them was his only hope of maintaining self-control.

Megan responded as if she could read his mind. She welcomed him but she matched his caution with her own. There was no tugging of his shirt, no more fumbling with the buttons. Her hands stayed discreetly above his waist. He kissed her and she kissed him back.

The moment wasn't as erotic as it was tantalizing. The feel of her mouth relaxed him, calmed him in ways he'd forgotten existed. He kissed her cheek and lowered his face against it, then traced the shell of her ear with his tongue.

"Goodness, Jody," she murmured, and slowly, the hands in his hair tightened; his scalp tingled. Lower, in that curve of his hip, he felt the curve of hers and the soft swell of her thigh. Heat began to radiate there.

He buried himself in the sweetness of her mouth, teasing, exploring, but increasingly plundering. He tried to hold back. Megan moaned and shifted under him. Caution! He felt the fight in her, so like his, and forced himself to concentrate on that. Even the fight felt good. Everything felt good. He'd had twenty-four hours of pleasure instead of headaches and heartburn. Every inch of him, every cell of his body was alive. Megan was there with him, against his body. It would have been so easy to let go and open the floodgates.

It was so much harder to keep them closed. Together, sharply, they pulled away from the kisses. Jody was quiet, commanding his respiratory system to slow down. Megan turned her face into his chest breathing deeply.

"Two sets of brakes are better than one," he murmured when he could.

Megan moaned, then laughed softly. He sat up but Megan was still lying down with her eyes closed. He glanced at her flushed face and heaving shoulders—exquisite torture.

After a long moment and a mental dousing with icy reprimands, Jody looked down at her again. She was bewildered, bemused and when she caught his eye, she smiled. "It's a darn good thing I brought you here and not to my apartment this weekend."

"Nobody's more surprised than I am," he replied.

They were quiet again. Megan sat up and rested her head against his shoulder. They both stared at the embers in the fireplace.

"Tell me about the Taft project being a lifeline, the bridge to the bogs."

"It's nothing. I don't know why I said that."

She was quiet.

He stroked her hair.

"You miss it, don't you, Jody?"

"Miss it?"

"The camaraderie, the closeness of working in a family business."

Was that it? "Maybe. As I get older, yes, I guess I do. I live so close—"

"And do so much for them, but it's not the same," she finished for him. "Not the same as being one of them."

"I was never one of them." Saints in heaven, where had that come from? Jody buried his face in his hands, then pushed them up, through his hair.

"Jody?"

He stood up. "I'm going to get some fresh air."

"You don't need fresh air, you need to finish what you were saying."

"I have finished." What had possessed him to begin? "I'm going for a walk."

"I'll go with you."

He put out his hand. "No. Stay here, Megan."

"Here! Not after all—"

"Go up to bed."

"And forget we ever talked? You're shutting me out."

"There's nothing more to say."

She was flushed and frustration kept her voice a whisper. "I thought we were having a conversation."

"We were. We did. Megan, I've said all there is to say."

Her expression told him how foolish he sounded. "You're shutting me out, but you're shutting yourself out, too, Jody, probably the way you always have."

"I'm not the gut-spilling type and I don't know why I said as much as I did."

"Because you need to talk about it. Can't you see that?"

He sighed. "At this moment, I can't see much of anything, not clearly anyway."

"Then for heaven's sake, don't go stumbling around out there in the dark trying to figure yourself out. Let me come, too. Don't push me away."

Jody put his hands on her shoulders. "Push you away? I just came within inches of carrying you out to the hayloft."

"I'm not talking about your hormones, I'm talking about your thoughts."

What did it matter? One was as disturbed as the other. He shook his head. "You're an incredible woman, Megan, but I need to be alone."

"Alone, that's all you've ever been. I'm still prying and you're still hedging."

"I'll see you in the morning." His tone was dismissive and the look in her eyes reflected it. Passion waned and self-preservation kicked in. Physically and emotionally he'd gone as far as he dared, maybe too far.

Nine

You're hedging; you're prying. I've never been one of them. As if the weekend were a diamond, Jody mentally examined facets of it as he traveled back to Massachusetts the following afternoon.

It wasn't until he was settled in his seat and the shuttle to Logan was underway that he gave himself the luxury of peeking at the Pandora's box in his head. He was pragmatic. He was a lawyer, he reminded himself, used to looking at life objectively.

The night before, when he'd left Megan, he'd walked in the dark under a pale moon, over Hugh O'Connor's rocky pasture, until the passion completely dissipated. It wasn't the passion that had kept him outside, however. It was the revelations. He wanted out of Hammell, Price and Bennett. He didn't want to fight other people's battles, even environmental ones.

He didn't want to go into politics. He didn't want to be governor. He wanted to go back to work the bogs.

Putting words to the torment was disconcerting. The fact that Megan had made him see it tied him in knots. Melt her heart! What about his? How could one disapproving redhead, in the course of twenty-four hours, turn his whole world inside out? Jody had paced in her father's pasture and looked back at the quiet house.

He'd only spilled his heart to her for Kevin and Erin's sake. He'd only meant to talk about them. He'd meant to talk sense to her. Yet it was she who gave shape to his nebulous yearnings, direction to his discontent. The idea was ludicrous, but there it was, in all its raw truth. He wanted to grow cranberries.

He was relieved when he'd returned to the house. She had gone up to bed, angry, no doubt, but no longer challenging. He'd said too much; the breath had been knocked out of him.

The next morning—this morning—with the self-control of a Spartan, he had managed to keep Hugh, chores and a meal wedged between himself and Erin's intriguing sister. She was distant in a way that made him ache, but it was a whole lot safer.

Their conversation centered on Megan's job and the possibilities in Millbrook. The three of them left for the airport in friendly, but hardly intimate spirits. He'd substituted a hug for a farewell kiss and the man Megan said goodbye to was as distracted as the one she'd found asleep on the hotel bed.

In one twenty-four-hour period he'd opened his inner self—albeit, a crack—to a complete stranger. Nearly a stranger. A stranger who knew him as well as he knew himself. A stranger who left him with a sense of calm as deep as his agitation. Megan O'Connor, the woman whose own professional life was unraveling, had pulled the lid from the pot he was stewing in, let the steam rise and put him back on simmer.

Now, cooled off and clearheaded, Jody was floating, adrift in uncharted waters without a compass. He shifted in his seat as the plane approached Boston. The wing dipped and the harbor glistened beneath him as the wind on the water splintered the reflected sun into a million fragments. Hardly more than an hour earlier, he'd hugged her, thanked her for the hospitality, been gracious when she'd thanked him for the interview. *See you at the wedding, keep me posted about the job situation...* Idle conversation. The hurt had still been in her eyes.

Pain radiated in his chest, a sort of sadness that swelled into desire and then drained into confusion. His body seemed to have a mind of its own and his head swam with memories of the pasture, the couch, the cows and the conversation.

He ached to know her chances of winding up at the radio station in Plymouth. Megan saw it as disaster. He didn't want—couldn't risk—any more soul-searching, but on another level, this one physical, he might be willing to risk quite a lot. He wasn't one for defining what he felt, but if he were, the word would have been "enchanted."

After a week away, Jody walked to the airport carpark, got into his Porsche and drove home. He arrived in Plymouth Sunday afternoon. Increasingly, the life he'd carved out for himself made for a tight schedule and a workload that often ceased being challenging and seemed simply heavy. *Megan knew it; she'd sensed it, she'd spoken of it.*

His condominium was the second floor of a renovated Saquish Street sea captain's house that still retained its panoramic view of the Plymouth anchorage, the breakwater and the bay beyond. His mail lay neatly piled on his desk, and a dinner was ready for his microwave oven, courtesy of Mildred Sousa, his housekeeper.

Jody put his briefcase on the desk and carried the mail and his suitcase into the bedroom. Bills, mostly. He changed from his traveling clothes and pulled on a favorite pair of khakis and a thick fisherman knit sweater to protect him from the biting wind coming off the sea. The marina was a healthy walk and with the exception of his meandering at Valley View, he'd had precious little exercise since he'd left for New York.

He did not, however, feel like being alone with his thoughts. Enchantment wasn't sitting well. He didn't feel like small talk with fellow sailors likely to be checking their crafts and he didn't feel like the company of neighbors he might run into at the corner pub and restaurant. Instead of walking down the steeply pitched sidewalk to the water, Jody got back into his car.

The Plymouth congestion thinned to outlying housing developments and finally to the expanse of pine forest and large country houses that marked the edge of his hometown. He took the long way, through the village proper. He passed the Millbrook Police Station on Pilgrim Street where Ryan had worked a second job to help defray Jody's undergraduate tuition.

Millbrook Common, bordered by handsome Georgian and Victorian houses, shops and the white-steepled church, split Main Street. Three doors down, Ryan's Bronco sat next to Sky's ancient Mercedes in the driveway of Schuyler House. At the far end of the grassy park, the fire station had its doors open. Sean's truck was in the lot; he was on duty. Even with the expense of building his own house for his wife and daughters, Sean, too, had kicked in for Jody when he could. "This ought to cover your books," he'd said, "with enough to take a coed to dinner once in a while."

Jody left the village. He followed Duxbury Road, past the land maintained by the Conservation Commission. It bordered a parcel of Bittersweet Bogs. Holly and Drew's first harvest had paid off part of Jody's law school loan.

Beyond the bogs, edging a golf course, Jody passed the sedate entrance to the Millbrook Country Club where teenage employee Ryan, always the town terror, had first challenged the irrepressible debutante Jane "Sky" Schuyler.

The last landmark was the medical clinic where Erin O'Connor, R.N., M.P.H., was Director of Women's Services. No more Harvard, no more Boston. Eight months earlier Matt had been sure she'd taken the position to be closer to Kevin. Megan thought so, too. Erin, Megan...family expectations. Jody was wrapped in them and sometimes it felt like tentacles.

His thoughts jumped from Branigan dreams for himself to O'Connor expectations for Erin. In the few years since Jody had passed the bar and entered his practice, all his older brothers had followed Sean into permanent relationships. Love hadn't come easily to any of them, not a single brother had done anything predictable and, with six of them, someone was always in a crisis.

For more than a year Jody had fought his vague feelings of discontent, smothered his restlessness un-

der grueling hours and exemplary legal work. He spent
his free time on his boat or ski slopes or with associates whose fast-paced lifestyles he emulated. None of
it gave him relief. That came from the work for the
bogs, hours heaped upon hours.

With family, he shared the good times easily, but
unlike any other Branigan, he carried the weight of his
self-doubts and increasing frustration alone. It was
impossible to turn to any of them because they were the
source of his success and, thus, the source of his pain.

The long, rutted driveway from the county road to
the Branigan houses wound through pines and stands
of birches. At the top of a small hill, the land opened,
first to the Greek revival antique that was Drew and
Holly's. Smoke curled from the chimney and a child's
wagon was on the grass.

Down the slope, bordering five acres of working
bogs, was the rambling farmhouse the men had grown
up in, separated from the storage barn and vegetable
garden by a courtyard. Jody parked his car between the
pickup truck neatly labeled Branigan Cranberries and
Kevin's cherry-red Corvette. Erin's old compact, now
a familiar sight, was also there.

Instead of heading for the house, Jody greeted the
panting family retrievers with a toss of a stick, and
started off along the dike bordering the rectangular
bogs. The tightness in his chest eased as he strolled over
the sandy work road. The atmosphere wouldn't be un-
familiar to Megan. He'd make a point to bring her out
here in July.

As he walked, his mind strayed, back to the first few
moments in the hotel room, back to lamplight and
peach silk, then teal-colored wool and wit. Megan

O'Connor, nearly a stranger, yet practically family, was already bound to him by that intimacy. Her opinions were as strong as her coffee and her aspirations as firm as her handshake. Just recalling their conversation revived the pleasure of her voice. What that woman could do with a simple sentence! His physical response heightened his color and he smiled, out on the dike by himself, reluctant to let go of the memory.

He cleared his thoughts and looked at the shadowed ditches and the scrubby plants and then at the pump house at the edge of the pond. It needed structural work and reshingling, and the engines supplying this set of sprinklers were in need of repair. Maintenance was constant and there were never enough hours or hands to get it all done.

Sean and Anne's house sat on the far side of the pond. There was a light on in the den and one upstairs in his niece's room. His older brothers all led separate lives, yet they were connected, by the seasons' rhythms, common goals, shared tasks. There, by himself, on the edge of the dike, he longed for that rhythm in his own life. His goals didn't jibe with the rest of theirs any more than his hours or his lifestyle. Isolation. Megan had noticed; it was just a matter of time before his associates did. He'd broached the unapproachable with Megan. It was time to do the same with Kevin. He wanted to come home.

Jody shoved his hands in his pockets and whistled for Max and Domino. The tightness in his chest returned; faint anxiety played in his gut as he strolled back towards the house. The sun was in the tops of the pines and Jody could see his brother under the light on the farmer's porch. Kevin whistled and the dogs trotted ahead. He hailed Jody and waved a greeting as his younger brother climbed the steps.

"Welcome back. I hear you stayed over an extra day and were treated to some O'Connor hospitality."

"Had to, for that interview Erin arranged. How'd you know?"

"Erin called home a while ago. I hope you worked on Megan. If ever we needed some heart-melting charm, it's now."

Jody frowned.

Kevin opened the door. "Have you got a minute?"

Jody nodded. "I was going to ask you the same thing. I need to talk with you."

"Perfect timing. I've got some things to tell you, as well." Kevin ushered him into the house.

Ten

Jody entered the kitchen and then the great room, both of which were empty. He watched the dogs settle at the wood stove and looked expectantly at his brother. "Where's Erin?"

They were equal in height and Kevin looked back at him. "Upstairs asleep. She feels lousy."

"Still? She had that bug before I left for New York! How did you manage to stay healthy?"

Kevin stayed on his feet. "As it turns out, it's not contagious."

"Is it serious?"

"Yes."

Jody's alarm turned to confusion as Kevin grinned. The older Branigan crossed the room and fed the stove.

Jody followed. "Kevin, talk to me, damn it. What is it?"

He dusted his hands. "It seems Erin's suffering from symptoms related to the first trimester of pregnancy. We're expecting."

"Expecting? Erin's pregnant?" Jody choked over his spontaneous laughter. "You? The one who lectured us behind the barn, the one who preached abstinence and protection from the time our voices dropped?"

"You sound like Ryan," he mumbled.

"I'll bet he got a hoot out of this. And Erin? She teaches family planning, for heaven's sake."

"Now you sound like Megan."

"That's why she called her sister?"

"I'll get to that if you'll let me finish."

Jody flopped onto the couch, all smiles. "Please do."

Kevin sighed and sat down. "The truth is, we were more—spontaneous—than we should have been, I guess. Erin's like that about everything, you know that."

"How's she taking it, besides throwing up?"

Kevin smiled again. "She's thrilled. With Holly pregnant, too, she thinks it's wonderful. I don't know what I've done to deserve her, but she swears it's exactly what she's wanted."

"And you?"

"Me." Kevin idly picked up a framed photograph from the side table. It was of Erin, in waders, harvesting cranberries the previous October, the day he'd proposed. He spoke to the picture. "We found out last Wednesday so I've had some time to let it sink in." The smile spread over his face and he looked back at Jody. "My God, I'm happy. It's a little soon, but I'd fill this house with our kids if she'd let me."

"You've never talked about having your own family."

"It was never in the cards for me. All of you were my family. Until Erin."

"What about the wedding?"

"That's why we called the farm. Obviously, plans have changed. We'll be married Saturday. Erin and I decided that since we can't pull this together the way we would have in July, it's going to be just immediate family, plus Nancy Reed who's been her roommate since college and a few others who've been close. Sky and Ryan are giving the reception and all the O'Connors will stay there. Matt will still be best man and Megan's still the maid of honor."

"Saturday!"

"That was Megan's reaction. She'll fly up with Hugh, and Bridget's driving down from New Hampshire."

"Did she go through the roof?"

"Bridget's thrilled. Megan, less so." The smile was gone and Kevin looked seriously at Jody. "It wasn't anything she said, it was more the absence of much enthusiasm. I know deep down, Megan always thought there'd be a chance this wouldn't work out, that her sister would see the light and call off the engagement. Now it's carved in stone."

Jody shrugged. "You've faced tougher criticism than hers."

"Hell, it doesn't bother me. It's Erin I worry about. No matter what her sister thinks, this is right for both of us. Hugh knows that, all of you know that. Erin's got everybody in her corner but Megan. You've met her, you're the most like her and I'm leaving it up to you to smooth things. I don't want Megan to ruin Erin's happiness."

Smooth things. If he only knew. Did he know? Jody shrugged. "Don't you think I tried this weekend? I talked myself blue in the face. I don't know what more I can do."

"You know her now. Keep at it, pound some sense into her. Whatever it takes, make her see the way things really are."

"The way things really are may be the problem," Jody joked. "But I'll try."

He wanted to close the conversation, afraid that his own weekend observations and behavior would tumble out. Had Megan disclosed anything to Erin? Was she likely to mention that Jody Branigan had nearly made love to her on her father's couch, that he'd talked of things he'd never discussed with anyone and admitted that he'd spent his whole professional life racing in the wrong direction?

Suddenly anxious to leave, he stood up. "I've got to get back. I've got hours of work ahead of me."

Kevin was glancing at the memorabilia in the comfortable room. "What was it you wanted to talk to me about?"

"You've got enough on your mind for the moment."

"Are you sure?"

"I'm sure. Concentrate on being the groom and getting the bride on her feet. My problems can wait." They would have to.

Kevin walked him back to the kitchen door. "Megan O'Connor's all yours, Jody. Start by calling her. She might be more receptive to a Branigan point of view on this latest development than she was to her sister's.''

"I've already given her a Branigan point of view," he shot back as he left for his car.

The walk on the bogs, the talk with Kevin had done him a world of good. It made him feel connected again. Back in Plymouth, Jody ate dinner alone and his mind wandered. Complications entrapped them all, but somewhere the gods were smiling. Make that laughing. Megan O'Connor was arriving in Millbrook on Friday.

For the first time in months, Jody was included in more than the legal goings-on of his family and he reveled in the familiar rhythm of organized chaos. To be a Branigan was to be an expert at crisis intervention.

Since Matthew lived in Boston, he was assigned to meet the O'Connor's plane. Friday afternoon there would be a wedding rehearsal and Kevin had managed to reserve a private dining room at the Millbrook Country Club for dinner afterwards. Sky had not only found caterers for the Saturday reception at Schuyler House, she also surprised the couple with the offer of her family home in Palm Beach for a honeymoon.

Anne and Sean Branigan were making arrangements for the few close friends who were being included. Holly took charge of the flowers. Ryan and Drew kept the family business running.

Through it all Erin went off to work at her medical clinic with a box of saltines and focused on coping with morning sickness, breaking the news to her associates and arranging a week's vacation for the impromptu honeymoon.

Jody's week was crammed with work and his evenings were crammed with Branigans. He put off the call to Megan until Wednesday to give her time to adjust to the news on her own. He got her apartment number from Erin and gave a lot of thought to what he would say. She answered on the second ring and her reply to his greeting was noncommittal.

"It seems you'll get that tour of Millbrook a little early."

"Don't expect me to pretend to be delighted."

"Now there's even more to celebrate."

Megan sighed and it drifted through him as he waited for her to speak. "No lectures, please, Jody. It's been a tough few days. You don't need to meet my plane. I haven't spoken with her yet, but if Sky can put me up for an extra night, I'm coming Thursday evening. I'll rent a car and drive down." Her voice was full of defeat and formality.

"Thursday? Wonderful! Don't bother with the rental. I'll be working at Government Center and I'll swing out to the airport and pick you up."

"I'll need a car in Millbrook."

"We've got plenty."

"I'd rather—"

"Megan!" She was silent and he followed his intuition. "Why Thursday? Is it more than the wedding?"

"Only my life." Her voice cracked. "It happened. I've been replaced."

The dead air between New Jersey and Massachusetts crackled with tension. Jody knew better than to expect sobs. Even sniffles would have been uncharacteristic. "The merger went through," he guessed.

"Tuesday afternoon."

"What about your demo?"

NO COST! NO OBLIGATION TO BUY! NO PURCHASE NECESSARY!

PLAY "LUCKY 7" AND GET AS MANY AS SIX FREE GIFTS ...

HOW TO PLAY:

1. With a coin, carefully scratch off the silver box at the right. This makes you eligible to receive one or more free books, and possibly other gifts, depending on what is revealed beneath the scratch-off area.

2. You'll receive brand-new Silhouette Desire® novels. When you return this card, we'll send you the books and gifts you qualify for *absolutely free*!

3. Unless you tell us otherwise, every month we'll send you 6 additional novels to read and enjoy. If you decide to keep them, you'll pay only $2.24* per book—that's 26¢ less per book than the cover price! And $2.24 per book is all you pay! There is **no** charge for shipping and handling. There are no hidden extras.

4. When you subscribe to Silhouette Reader Service™, we'll also send you additional free gifts from time to time, as well as our newsletter.

5. You must be completely satisfied. You may cancel at any time simply by writing "cancel" on your statement or returning a shipment of books to us at our cost.

She laughed sarcastically. "They loved it. I taped David on Monday and edited half the night. It was presented yesterday as an example of my creativity. It saved me, to their way of thinking."

Jody proceeded gingerly, buoyed by the fact that they were focusing on her problems, not his. "I'm sure it was excellent."

"Whether it was or wasn't, we're now one of five affiliate stations of Reinbach Communications of Chicago. My position here is being filled by their director from Illinois. They did offer me the chance to set up a similar position at the Plymouth station."

His heart jumped. He looked through the window as if to find those laughing gods hovering on the other side of the mullions.

"Jody?"

"I'm still here, fighting the urge to comment on fate. Your father's delighted?"

"Of course."

"And you're devastated."

"Yes. The irony of this whole mess is painfully obvious so don't get all smug and self-righteous."

"Never. Besides, this gives you a chance to start from scratch and really show them what you can do. You'll have to relocate, but that's not uncommon in your line of work. It doesn't sound so bad."

"I feel like a dog being thrown a bone."

"Have you thought of leaving the group? Have you interviewed anywhere else?"

"Of course. There's nothing here, nothing in the metropolitan area. Nothing!" The strength returned to her voice. "Friday I'll take a look at WJQG. I'm planning to take the position temporarily, six months, whatever's reasonable."

"Until something better comes along."

"Yes. Finding something while employed is a heck of a lot easier than being out of work and looking."

"You're not one to burn your bridges. Does Erin know?"

"I'm going to call her as soon as we hang up." After another pause, Megan added, "You haven't told them anything about this?"

"You asked me not to."

"Thank you, Jody."

"Megan, have you discussed—" He was going to say us, but it sounded ridiculous. "—me, the weekend, with Erin?"

She didn't reply immediately. Finally, Jody heard her sigh. "The way it ended, the way you pulled back . . . No. Your problems are your own. Isn't that the way you wanted it?"

"Yes. I appreciate it."

"While there was still a chance that my job was secure here, I thought it would be smart to forget anything ever happened. Except for the wedding, we'd barely see each other anyway."

Her words slapped at him. "But now?"

"Now, I'm going to be right under your nose. But I don't have time to straighten out your life while I'm pulling mine from the ashes. No more prying."

The mood had lightened enough so that her tone of voice was friendly, anxious. Jody matched her sincerity with his own. "Good. I want to help, Megan."

"Odd as it sounds, I'd like that. I suspect you're better at fixing other lives than you are at patching up your own."

"You'll be fine, Megan. Life doesn't always work out according to Plan A. Just ask your sister. Be thankful there's a Plan B."

"Small favors."

"Do one for me," he replied.

"What?"

"Let me meet your plane."

Eleven

Occasionally things went according to plan in Branigan lives, even if it turned out to be Plan B. As scheduled, Jody was in Boston on Thursday, this time on behalf of the South Shore Lobstermen's Association. He left the Saltonstall Building, inched his Porsche through the traffic in the Callahan Tunnel and crawled to Logan Airport. He was late.

She was standing outside the terminal with a single suitcase and a large briefcase. The wind off Boston Harbor flattened her trench coat against her and she brushed her hair away from her face with a gloved hand. She looked annoyed and cold and as appealing as ever.

Jody drove to the curb and opened the passenger door, enjoying her surprise as she looked the car over. "Welcome to spring in New England."

"You should have warned me."

"And risk your choosing unemployment instead of Plymouth? No way!" A commuter bus roared past as he put her luggage in the trunk. He stopped with his hands on the open trunk lid as he looked at her. Megan's blue eyes were haunting. She closed them slowly as if she had a headache, and he watched her lashes brush her cheek. Her face was pink from the wind but the vibrancy so evident in New Jersey was gone. He closed the trunk and put his arm around her shoulder, walking her protectively to the passenger door. Amidst the fumes and the noise, they drove off.

The road south to Millbrook was no more pleasant than the hop from Government Center into East Boston. When Megan commented on the typical traffic and endless construction, Jody smiled. "You might have managed it alone, but it wouldn't have done a thing for your mood. Now sink back against the headrest and let someone else take charge."

She obeyed and said to the ceiling, "There's nothing wrong with my mood and I won't ruin Erin's weekend, if that's what you're worried about."

"What makes you think I'm worried?"

"You keep frowning at me."

Jody let it pass. Once south of Boston he turned on the radio. "WJQG. Good little station. About to get even better."

"Jody, I'm in no mood—" She stopped. "Never mind."

"What a difference a few days can make," he replied. "Not getting much sleep?"

"I've had a lot on my mind." There was no argument in her voice.

"Frantic days, what with all those last-ditch efforts to find another job around New York in your free time?"

"Yes, frantic days. Miserable days." She'd said it so softly he regretted his teasing.

"Hasn't left much time for David Howell, either."

She looked at him curiously. "I've managed to see him this week," she shot back. "You don't look pleased. I got a great interview."

Jody turned quickly to meet her gaze and then looked back at the road, damning himself for bringing it up as if he were a jealous teenager. "Megan, you need moral support in all this and frankly, you don't look as though you've gotten much."

He sensed the slip in her composure. As he drove, Megan took a deep breath and looked again at the ceiling of the Porsche. After a pause she replied, "Whatever might have happened with David won't, given the distance."

The weight in his chest lifted. "And your father?"

"Sympathy's the furthest thing from his mind. My father thinks all this is wonderful. After graduation, Bridget wants to break into advertising in Boston. It's a little easier than New York, obviously. Now he'll have all of his daughters up here with six of you to look after us. You'll excuse me if I don't consider that ideal."

Jody smiled. "Only if you'll excuse me for thinking it's a very pleasant assignment."

The woman who'd led him in a two-day battle of wills was quiet. The week's events had rearranged her personal and professional life so completely that her attempts at bravado were useless. "I don't need any man looking after me."

"Then I'll try to do it unobtrusively. Megan, all you've discovered is that life's road has ruts after all. If there's one thing I've learned from your sister, it's that O'Connors go after what they want with the same determination that Branigans do."

"Let's leave Erin out of this and discuss Branigans as little as possible."

Beside him, this new Megan suddenly seemed very vulnerable and his heart went out to her.

"Are you ready for Sky's?" Jody snapped off the radio. "It's four o'clock. I can take you there, out to Kevin and Erin's at the bogs, or we can tour Millbrook while you gather your courage and all this sinks in."

Megan put her gloved hand over her eyes. The kid leather trembled. "Not yet. I'm so tired... Everything's happened so fast. It's been a hellish week." She looked at him. "Jody, isn't there someplace else, just for a little while?"

"There sure is, Megan. I'll take you home."

At Saquish Street, he took her suitcase and ushered her into his bedroom, suggesting a change of clothes. They were back to square one, emotionally and without the focus on him. Jody was elated.

There wasn't much other than chowder in the refrigerator, but while she was changing, he heated up the last of it. Over the scraping of his wooden spoon along the bottom of the pan, he listened to the muffled sounds from the next room. As the chowder simmered, so did he. Megan came into the kitchen in slacks and a fleece shirt as he was breaking up lettuce for a salad.

"You shouldn't have," she said as she walked toward him. It felt good just to look at her.

She continued to protest. "You don't need to feed me. I could have grabbed something. We could have gone out."

Jody finished and wiped his hands. "Megan, last weekend may have gotten a little heavy, but you prescribed exactly what I needed. Give me the chance to return the favor. Let me get into something comfortable, too, and then we'll eat." He meant to pass by her, but she turned to him and as he watched, her blue eyes darkened.

He put his hands out, first to her shoulders and then on either side of her face. She looked up at him with a wide and pensive expression and slowly opened her hands against his shirt.

"I hate this," she murmured.

"Destiny, of course, not me."

She laughed. "How about life at the bottom of the communications ladder?"

"It's a good place to start." He was rekindled. Had he thought he wouldn't be? The intimacy of the moment washed over him as she slid her hands around him and pressed herself into a hug. He put his arms across her back and she rested against him, cheek, breasts, hips and legs, upright, not prone, but it felt just as good. He held her, unwilling or unable to break the spell. It didn't matter.

She shifted and as she raised her head, Jody kissed her. As always the match was perfect, the pressure intense. He parted her lips, welcoming the ache that shot into every fiber of his body. She wasn't just a woman, she was Megan.

She responded and the soft, gentle pressure against him strengthened. "Jody," she murmured, tearing herself from the kiss and settling back into the hug.

He held her against him again and caressed her hair. "Would you consider complicating things?"

"More?" She smiled and answered dreamily, "Not even if you were someone else. But this feels wonderful."

"But?"

"You know the but. I have my life to unscramble and you're sinking in your own quagmire."

"Is that how you see it!"

"My impressions are from you, Jody."

"And unlike your sister, you know when to put on the brakes."

She considered his comment. "I don't deny that Erin thinks she's doing the right thing."

"There's that but again. But if she'd had your control things would be different."

"You can't deny it."

"I could, but we've argued enough about your sister and my brother." Jody shifted. "We've argued enough about everything. If you want me in control, I'd better concentrate on the chowder instead of those blue eyes." He tapped her forehead. "There's somebody in there with a new life ahead of her, Megan."

"That's what I'm afraid of." She picked up the spoon and stirred the chowder.

Perfect body, gorgeous green eyes, she'd said about him, back on her own territory. He was driving himself crazy. Though there'd been precious little melting of her heart, he feared for his own. Megan O'Connor buoyed his spirits and challenged his wit. Her convoluted personality intrigued him. Until he met her, he hadn't met a woman who'd ever made him think beyond the moment.

They sat at his table. "Megan, give this a chance.
The pace at Valley View is similar to the bogs: hard
work, long hours, good food and comfortable beds.
Simple pleasures. I know that's what you're trying to
get away from, but once you're here, you might find it
a comfort sometimes."

"I've endured one too many jokes about the farmer's
daughter to think of Deans Corner as anything more
than a life I've outgrown. Farming of any sort has no
appeal. I suppose that's what all those brothers hoped
for you, that it wouldn't be appealing."

"Finish your chowder."

"Coward," she whispered, but she was smiling.

After the meal she looked at photographs of his
boat, and Jody drew her a map with directions from
Sky's to the WJQG station. What he ached for, he
didn't dare suggest, and as the sun set, Jody drove her
through the dusky Plymouth streets out of town and
into Millbrook. It was startling how easily she fit in his
life, how he forgot the stressful days and dreamed of
her at night.

Twelve

As Jody entered Millbrook proper, Megan commented on the charm of the village.

"New England at its most seductive, I hope." He pointed out the carriage house Erin had been renting on the Morgan property.

"I'm going to sublet it, I guess. She'll even throw in some furniture since your brother's house is furnished."

"Believe me, there will be room for Erin's touch at the house. Keep your mind open," he added as they pulled into the Schuyler House driveway.

He enjoyed her response to Sky's family house. Jody pulled her luggage from the trunk and watched her admire the classic Georgian lines of the stately historic home.

"I had no idea," she murmured.

"It's been in her father's family since it was built. She used to summer here and two years ago she came back to restore it. She restored her relationship with my brother at the same time."

"He was a police officer then?"

"Yes. It paid most of my graduate school tuition."

"You owe your brothers quite a bit, don't you, Jody?"

"Everything I am, Megan."

"There's the problem," Megan replied as Sky swung open the wide front door.

The attorney in him kicked in automatically. He chose to ignore her remark and watched the women greet each other. The old Megan surfaced, the one saved for the world. She was as gracious and pleasant as Sky, and offered not a hint of the fatigue or confusion that had nearly unraveled her. Hard to believe that the sophisticate making small talk had been in his arms, all dewy-eyed and overwhelmed.

Jody's brother appeared on the staircase in gray flannel slacks and an oxford cloth shirt. Sky had on a woman's equivalent, softened by a silk scarf and kid slippers.

Ryan took Megan's luggage upstairs and Sky, insisting that Jody stay for dessert, headed back through the butler's pantry. Megan's surprise made Jody laugh. When they were alone, he whispered, "You were expecting hip boots, overalls and flannel shirts. I hope you're not disappointed." He was delighted when she blushed.

Until Sky returned, the suddenly demure Megan glanced at what she could see of the museum quality furniture in the oversized rooms and then the four of them went into the library.

Small talk turned quickly to the wedding plans, but as Sky and Megan became engrossed in the details, Ryan brought up the bogs. The men moved to the desk where Ryan pulled out photocopied projections on an Integrated Pest Management experiment on the small parcel of bogs at Drew and Holly's.

"Look it over when you get a minute. I can't make sense of the last four pages. If you've got time after the wedding, maybe Sunday, we can take a look at Holly's system. She thinks she's got it under control, but I don't know how she'll find the time once the baby comes."

"She's probably got more time than I do," Jody mused, as he turned the pages and skimmed the legalese.

Ryan put his hand on his brother's shoulder. "There's more. Drew's stewing over the Taft proposal for the Conservation Commission."

Jody studied Ryan. "It's a gamble. He knows it and so do the rest of you. Conservation Commission, state EPA, federal EPA, DEQE... He's not the only one doing the stewing."

"He doesn't expect things to happen overnight."

"Good! There's not much chance of that," Jody snapped.

Ryan went back to Sky and Megan while Jody stayed at the desk, perusing the file. Megan asked and Ryan explained what Jody was handling for his brothers. She shot him a studied look.

"The paperwork alone looks staggering," she said.

Ryan laughed. "Keeps him out of trouble."

Jody listened to them from the desk. Listened to *her*. Megan's voice and her animated conversation drifted over, breaking his concentration. He turned as she talked with his brother. She was discussing her up-coming interview with the Providence station and there was finally a hint of enthusiasm in her voice.

Jody stayed across the room in the hard-backed desk chair and watched. The lamp on the end table threw light across her shoulder, illuminating her profile and highlighting her flaming hair. She leaned forward, gesticulating as she described the frustration of her professional situation. Ryan said something that made her laugh and she leaned back into the couch, com-fortable and relaxed.

Jody turned back to his work. This was the Megan she wanted the world to see, sophisticated, urbane, in control of her destiny—the woman who had emerged from out of his dream at the foot of his hotel bed.

What of the Megan she'd left behind? Jody laughed, too, but not at Ryan. There was a very appealing side to her he'd forever associate with rocky green pas-tures, Holsteins and grazing sheep. The one who'd left him breathless at Valley View. That was the Megan he wanted back in his arms, under him, enfolding him. No soul-searching, no heartrending, just the sound of his name deep in her throat and the touch of her hands in his hair.

"Jody?"

His spine stiffened as she touched his shoulder.

"Be finished in a minute."

He picked up the file and Megan tilted her head and looked down at him. Never would he tire of those blue eyes! Few moments in the hectic week had given Jody as much pleasure as these. The fates were being gen-erous. There, in his sister-in-law's library, with her hand on his shoulder, was the personification of dis-traction. She was the adrenaline rush, the pounding heart, the longing, the complications too deep to fathom. He wanted her living in Millbrook. He wanted her in his arms, in his bed, in his life. To hell with the complications!

Sky was arranging the loan of a Branigan car for the following day and pressing Megan to consider renting Erin's carriage house as Jody reluctantly said goodbye. All three of them walked him to the door, which only increased his desire to be alone with Megan.

"Call me at the office and let me know how the interview goes," was the most intimate thing he dared to say.

"If I get a minute, I will," was all the reply he got.

Don't complicate things. How he ached to do just that. Jody left the three of them in the big, comfortable house and drove the dark back roads to the harbor. She'd accepted the assignment for six months. It was as close to forever as he wanted to think about.

Friday morning Jody took the Branigan files with him to the office. He was at his desk by seven-thirty, but still didn't have much time for family business. He was popping antacids by midmorning and washing them down with the usual coffee, all the while forcing himself not to anticipate a call from Megan. At one o'clock, while he was speaking on the phone with a lobsterman, feet on his desk, legal pad in hand, she breezed through his door.

He motioned to a chair and concluded the seafaring business as she sat down, crossed her legs and pulled a thread from the sleeve of her jacket. It was ultrasuede and he watched her fingers as she brushed the fabric. Even her fingers incited a rush.

The moment he hung up the phone, Megan held up a paper plate with a half-eaten doughnut and his open roll of antacids. "This was breakfast?"

"Lunch, actually. How was the interview? Want some coffee?"

"Fine. No, thank you. Don't change the subject. This is a miserable excuse for lunch. Jody, how can you eat this sorry substitute for food? With the pressure you're under, you'll give yourself an ulcer or a heart attack."

"I appreciate your concern." He lifted his feet off the desk and swiveled to face her. "If I promise to eat a tossed salad and a bran muffin tomorrow will you tell me what you thought of the station?"

"Tomorrow's the wedding."

"Unless you speak up when the priest asks if anyone objects."

"That was unfair."

He grinned. "Was it?"

She shifted. "I think we've run the subject into the ground. I didn't come over here to rehash my feelings about Erin."

"And the Branigans."

Megan sighed and glanced out the window as if collecting her thoughts. "Jody, don't you see how they pressure you? We couldn't even have dessert last night without Ryan throwing a file of legal rigmarole at you. Kevin and Drew just expect you to take on whatever needs to be done."

Jody considered the implications. "You've been discussing me?"

Megan tossed her head. "You left too soon last night. Kevin and Erin and Drew came over. They all seemed interested in my reaction to you."

"You might as well include me in that category."

"You make me crazy, Jody. Your body's magnificent. I wish I knew as much about the workings of your brain."

She said it so fast, he sat up in his chair.

Megan pointed at him. "Don't get me off the subject. I told them you were half-dead when I met you last weekend. Anyone can see the stress you're living with, anyone but a Branigan."

"I'm flattered. However, I don't imagine they agreed with you about stress."

"They were more interested in hearing about the condition you were in when I woke you up in your hotel room."

Jody groaned. "You didn't tell them what I was wearing."

Megan smiled and then chuckled as she nodded. "They're family, after all. It seems a few years ago you met Holly half-naked while zipping yourself into jeans."

"Drew came charging into the room with her." Jody's ears began to burn. "Remind me not to leave you alone with them for the duration of the weekend."

She grew serious. "They love you, Jody, but their expectations are as overwhelming as their respect. There's no room for failure."

"Awe inspiring, isn't it."

"I'm serious."

Jody sat there at a rakish angle in his swivel chair and watched her. It was incredibly arousing to think that she'd discussed him, analyzed his situation, considered the life he was leading, *found his body magnificent*.

Thirteen

—

It played havoc with his hormones. "Save your grumbling. Is it me you're really worried about or Erin?"

She was thoughtful. "Erin's happy, Jody. I can see that."

"Let her have that happiness. She doesn't want your worry and I don't need it."

Megan stood up and her glance held his. "That remains to be seen. For now, though, you're right."

"Especially with your own life such a shambles," he finished for her. "Did you take the job?"

"Yes, for the time being. I don't see much choice."

"How soon do you start?"

"Whenever I can make the switch. I told them the end of the month."

"How about living arrangements?"

"It seems foolish not to take Erin's apartment." His heart sang while her eyes clouded. "I hate this. I don't have control of anything anymore!"

He went to her, shaking his head. "You're not lost, Megan. It's a situation that's been forced on you, that's all. Keep an open mind. You can set the world on fire from Millbrook, if you want to."

"I don't know what I want anymore."

"A temporary situation, I assure you. Settle down, get your bearings. You'll be full of fight again in no time."

"Is that how you see me, recalcitrant, full of fight?"

"Does it matter how I see you, Megan?" He touched the suede and brushed it slowly with both hands open on her arms.

"It might."

Jody watched her. She closed her eyes and he looked at her mouth before leaning forward. Her lips were warm under his and when he traced them with his tongue, she moaned softly.

She opened her hands against his chest. "Thunder, again. Your heart's pounding," she whispered.

He played with her hair and covered her fingers with his free hand. "You're trembling."

They kissed again and he wove patterns against her tongue with his. Megan moved against him slowly, as if they were dancing, and her warmth made him ache. He didn't dare touch her anywhere else. Even as he kissed her, he put space between them and with a final sigh, he stepped back.

"Megan—"

She put her hand up. "It was just a kiss."

Jody touched her outstretched fingers and barely above a whisper he said, "The hell it was."

She pulled her hand back gently. "You're a lawyer and you'll tie me in verbal knots. Please don't complicate things by talking."

Jody smiled. "That's my line."

"I'm glad you can admit it. For you words, feelings seem to be the ultimate complication." Megan cleared her throat but her eyes stayed bright. "For me, it's this dependence."

"You don't like it."

"Depending on you? Quite the contrary. I like it very much. It'll make this transition easier. Erin's all tied up in her own happiness and her own problems. It would be very unfair of me to lean on her this spring. It's a wonderful feeling knowing that I can count on you."

"But?"

"You're a man and I'm a woman and we shouldn't confuse this initial rush of feelings with anything deeper."

Counselor Branigan was nothing if not quick on his feet. "You've admitted to discussing me with my family. You've fussed over everything from my nutritional intake to my work load. Now you're worried that I might misconstrue the way you respond to me physically?"

"You're teasing."

He shrugged. "You think it's a wonderful feeling knowing you can count on me, but I shouldn't consider the possibility that there might be anything more serious?"

"Really, Jody!"

He kissed her forehead. "Wonderful. You know my schedule, I don't have time for anything serious." He thought better of adding what he did have time for.

Megan looked at her watch. "Good, I feel better. I've kept you long enough. Bridget's driving down from school this afternoon and we're spending the rest of the day with Erin. I'll see you tonight, of course."

Jody smiled. "I'm looking forward to it." He watched her walk to the door. "Megan?"

"Hmmm?"

"Your blouse is untucked." He was hoping for a flustered expression but she smiled, smoothed it and opened the door.

"Jody, darling, you've got lipstick on your chin."

That night he was the last to arrive at the Millbrook Country Club. He'd taken his time, anticipating an onslaught of family business discussions from all sides. During the solitary ride from Plymouth, he'd reviewed the points he needed to discuss with Holly and Drew regarding their bog conversation. By the time he'd finished reading the proposal and sorting through the requirements the night before, it had been after midnight, due to his lack of concentration as much as the work.

The dinner was in a private dining suite on the second floor of the club. Jody appeared at the door as hors d'oeuvres were being passed around. The room was a sea of family, including the wedding party. His five dark-haired, fair-complexioned brothers and the redheaded father of the bride were interspersed with Branigan wives and O'Connor sisters. It made a staggeringly handsome portrait.

Jody answered various welcomes and scanned the group with anticipation prickling his skin. He found her in the corner, standing with Drew and Ryan. Megan was dressed in knee-weakening black fabric that fell gently from her shoulder across her breasts and again from her hips to her knees. Long sleeves capped her wrists. Her flaming hair was pulled back over one ear with a black satin bow, leaving the rest to fall along the side of her face. Watching her nearly drained him of all rational thought.

He took one enormous breath and looked from Megan to Erin to Bridget to Hugh. Then he scanned the faces of his own family. He hoped it would pound some sense into him. Megan O'Connor was already connected to his heart and come tomorrow, unseverable ties would bind them.

How much easier, simpler—less painful, no doubt— a platonic friendship would be. The inner voice fell on deaf ears. This woman was worth tempting fate. The moment he caught her eye, she smiled, pulled two champagne glasses from the nearest tray and started across the room. The matte finish of her dress absorbed the light, increasing tenfold the contrast with her skin. Her hair shone and the draped fabric clung, then fell away from her body as she came to him.

Megan handed him a glass and raised the other. "My father's going to propose a toast in a moment. We've been waiting for you."

"I'll hold that thought."

She smiled and looked at her sister. Color washed her cheeks and the implication that it was from his presence threatened what was left of his composure. Hugh spoke, then Kevin took over and by the time the toasts were completed, the strength had returned to Jody's knees.

The party was seated at a banquet table with Hugh at one end and Kevin at the other. Jody had Sky on his left, Bridget O'Connor on his right. Megan sat directly across from him as if to symbolize the weekend: so close and yet so far. With powers of concentration he didn't know he had, Jody turned, introduced himself to Bridget and asked about her career plans.

After dinner and an array of family anecdotes, the Branigans and O'Connors lingered over coffee, still engrossed in knots of conversation. Every time Jody felt Megan's glance from across the table, it threw his fantasies into high gear. The frustration of having her just out of reach was tempered only by the encouragement he felt as he watched her talk pleasantly with Drew and Ryan who sat on either side of her.

The party broke up amidst reminders that two households had baby-sitters with curfews and there was a bride present who needed more than her usual amount of sleep.

Jody looked at Ryan. "I'll drive Megan over." In his peripheral vision he caught the blur of red hair as she snapped her attention to him. Her high color was back, but whatever protest she might have made went unspoken.

"Ryan had room," she said moments later, as they left the club and got into his car.

"It wasn't a matter of room."

Megan lowered her voice. "No, I didn't think it was. You shouldn't have done this."

"You could have turned me down."

"And have all those brothers raising their eyebrows up into their hairlines? No thank you."

He laughed and started the car. "Enjoy the attention. Want to go parking? I have a few favorite haunts out here."

"I'll bet you do. Schuyler House, please. I don't want our families speculating on anything where you and I are concerned."

"Am I allowed to speculate?"

He glanced sideways and caught her Cheshire cat smile as she leaned back into the seat, bathed in shadows. "Haven't you been speculating all night, Counselor?"

He looked back at the road. "Haven't you?"

Her laughter filled the Porsche. It was soft, throaty, provocative beyond bearing. With Ryan and Kevin behind him, he entered Millbrook via Pilgrim Street, pulled onto Main and then ducked into the first driveway. Megan sat up as the cars continued past and stopped half a block beyond.

"This isn't Sky's!"

"No, it's the Morgans', the carriage house you'll be renting. The others will just think you're having a look at where you'll be living."

"Jody!"

"Would you prefer that I kiss you senseless down the street with your father, sisters and two of my brothers watching?"

"I would prefer that you not kiss me senseless at all."

He leaned closer. Megan was completely relaxed. He touched her and rather than pull away, she leaned toward him. He stroked her hair. "Do you mean it?"

She shook her head.

"I've wanted to do this since I walked in the room tonight."

"Can you promise no more than a kiss?" she whispered.

"Yes," he murmured, already covering her mouth with his. He would have promised anything for the feel of her against his palms and the tumble of hair against his cheek. His eyes were closed and Megan cupped his face with her hands. Her fingers felt cold against his overheated skin. The smooth black jersey, beyond his touch all night, was warm and yielding. He plundered her mouth and she matched him until her own erratic breathing forced her breasts against his hands.

"Jody," was barely more than a whisper.

Self-control ebbed as waves of desire built in him and Megan succumbed. "I don't know how you do it, but you make me forget everything else. Everything."

She sighed against him, her hand in his hair. "Tell me what it is you want to forget, Jody. I'd like to listen."

"Someday."

He couldn't talk, didn't want to, didn't need to. He needed her mouth back on his. He needed the teasing trail of her kisses on his jaw and her fingers in his hair. She obliged with a force that swept him away from reality.

They separated while they were still able. He forced himself to move away. "Damn it, we aren't teenagers sitting in your father's driveway. It's time to get you home." With a rueful laugh he rested his head on the steering wheel. "You cannot imagine what it takes for me to say that."

"Yes, I think I can." Megan took his hand and brought it to her breast. He groaned again and beneath his fingertips he felt the heartbeat and her straining pebble-hard nipple.

She slid her hand inside his sports jacket and skimmed two fingers between the buttons of his dress shirt. "Yours, too."

His, too, and if Megan had so much as worked one button through its hole, he would have continued. There in the bucket seats, inside the carriage house, on Saquish Street. It didn't matter where.

Megan didn't unbutton anything. She took a lapel in each hand and drew the blazer together. "Wasn't I just talking about this infatuation of ours back at your place last night?"

"Is that what it is?"

"Jody, I'll be darned if I have a clue."

As he turned the ignition on, she combed her hair and refastened the bow. In less than a minute they were in the proper driveway where Kevin was getting into his Corvette. As Jody caught him in his headlights, he waved but didn't stop.

"A true gentleman," Megan said, her voice still shaky. "I'm sure he suspects."

"He has other things on his mind."

"So should we." She sat still for a moment, her head back, eyes closed. He didn't interrupt. Finally, as Megan opened her door, she turned to face him. "I'm as much to blame as you are, but this can't happen again. If you value our friendship, Jody, make me a promise."

With his index finger he traced a line from her shoulder to her heart. "I promise, Megan, that there'll be no more front seat foolishness, no more stolen kisses. The next time I kiss you—"

She pressed her fingers over his mouth. "Don't finish that."

"I'm not one to leave anything unfinished."

"Some things are better left alone."

"Not us, Megan." Kevin had gone and Jody followed her from the car to the house. A light shone over the door and she stepped beyond it, into the shadows.

"There's still time to be rational," she added.

"I've tried that line on myself all night. In fact I've been repeating it since I left you last Sunday. Maybe since I kissed you among the cows and the sheep." He looked past her, to the deserted street. "Maybe since I found you at the end of my bed."

"Foolishness."

"Damn right."

"Good night, Jody."

"Good night, Megan."

Fourteen

The late April afternoon cooperated. Never balmy in New England, it was at least bright, full of promise and sunshine. After a fitful night alone in Plymouth and a stab at work, Jody dressed as they all would, in a blazer and slacks. His were conservatively cut, expensively made and fit him perfectly.

He drove out to the house he'd grown up in and found Kevin teasing Matt about Bridget's interest in him. They were in the kitchen and Matt was systematically denying any chemistry.

"Had a visitor this morning," Kevin said as he straightened his tie.

Jody patted the dogs. "Bridget?"

Kevin shook his head. "Megan. Gave her a tour."

Unaccountably, Jody felt the heat in his cheeks. "Did you?"

"You, too?" Kevin mused.

"Me, too, what?"

"You tell me. Why're you pink?"

Jody pulled open the refrigerator. "Forget it."

"Don't get Kevin started," Matt broke in. "The groom's on an O'Connor kick."

"I thought Megan was the enemy," Jody said from the depths of the milk tray.

"Unless I'm mistaken, she's mellowing, or maybe it's just that her mind's on another Branigan."

Jody stepped back from the refrigerator and looked at him sharply. "I've just been following orders."

"At Sky's the other night, after you'd left, we all got an earful about you and the pressure you're under. Maybe she's right. After the Taft project comes up before the board, back off for a while. We can get along without you."

"How well I know."

"You have a problem with that?"

Jody shrugged. "Kevin, let me decide how much work I can handle."

"I want you to back off. It's putting too much pressure on you."

"Let me be the judge of that!" He changed the subject abruptly. "I'm surprised Megan was interested in a tour."

Kevin was in no mood to argue either. "She told me it was for Erin's sake. We'll never make a cranberry grower out of her."

"If she liked farming, she'd be back in Deans Corner with the Holsteins," Jody said.

"I get the feeling you've made an impression on her."

"Good. That's what I intended to do." He found it necessary to busy himself with the dog dishes.

Kevin was smiling. "If it's all for my benefit, thanks. However, I suspect you're discovering that O'Connor women have a way of getting under your skin, whether you want them to or not."

Jody stood up. "The last thing on Megan's mind is a cranberry grower."

"You're not one."

Inexplicably, the comment stabbed. Jody let it pass. "Even if I were interested in her, I don't have the time to figure her out."

"Might be worth the effort, for both of you."

"Cool the fatherly advice," Matt threw in.

Kevin grinned. "Two of you and two of them."

"Spoken by a man just minutes from the altar who can't bear to have bachelors left in the family."

Kevin simply shook his head. "You should be so lucky."

The wedding ceremony was beautiful in its simplicity. Over the gentle strains of the organist's Handel, the families and friends assembled in the front pews. As they came from the robing room, Jody watched Matt and Kevin, the first and last of his brothers.

The more ensconced in law Jody became, the more he marveled at Matt's dedication to medicine and his brother's ability to do everything right. It added guilt to his discontent and for years that guilt had spurred his determination to live up to Kevin's expectations. Familiar symptoms began to surface and Jody pressed a fist against his stomach as the music stopped.

Rather than progress down the long, empty aisles, the bride's attendants came from the sacristy, to the left of the altar. A Bach cantata drifted from the organ as Jody's nieces appeared with baskets of flowers. He leaned over and winked at Drew's toddler Maria and then, as he straightened up, Megan appeared.

She was dressed in pale yellow silk that fit as provocatively as the black jersey had, or maybe it was that anything on Megan O'Connor looked provocative. Three tiger lilies in her bouquet matched her hair and even those took on sensuous overtones. Jody didn't stop to analyze; he simply stood and enjoyed it.

If he were being a fool, he was a happy fool. Erin, on her father's arm, appeared last. She, too, had on a street-length silk dress, a shade darker than her sister's. The color of sunshine, Jody thought as he tried to read Megan's thoughts.

Kevin took Hugh's place and the vows were exchanged. Erin's voice was clear, lilting, full of happiness, but Kevin's shook. Heads turned as Matt, who had already handed the groom the ring, gave him a handkerchief. Kevin stopped and pressed it against his eyes.

The scene touched Jody's heart and he watched the maid of honor. Megan looked amused, then startled, then, for a moment, as if emotion might overwhelm her, too. What was clearest of all, however, was affection.

When the ceremony ended, the entire group strolled across the common for the reception at Schuyler House. After the formal photographs had been taken, Jody wandered through the first floor, making idle conversation as he went. Matt assembled them all in the front parlor, which gave Jody the excuse to lift two champagne glasses from the caterer's tray and hand one to Megan. She stood quietly next to him as the best man raised his glass and the crumpled handkerchief.

"Proof," he told the guests, "Superman is human after all."

Kevin tried to snatch it but Erin pulled his arm down. Hugh O'Connor raised his glass. "One last toast. To the O'Connors and the Branigans, joined now by love and devotion. May Kevin and Erin's own children prosper from the same love Kevin has already given his brothers."

"They'll be perfect, Hugh," Kevin replied. "I got the kinks out by practicing on this bunch."

There was soft laughter and next to Jody, Megan sipped her champagne. "Are you all right?" he asked.

She nodded. "You're a surprising bunch."

"The bigger they are, the more they need someone like your sister," he replied.

"Maybe so. Erin doesn't have a doubt in the world."

"Has your time with her convinced you she's doing the right thing?"

Megan nodded. "Yes. I should admit that for Erin it does seem right."

For Erin, repeated itself in Jody's head.

With Megan next to him, Jody looked through the mullioned windows and back across the common. "My parents were married over there in that little church. Their funeral was there, too. Kevin never went back except for Peter Bancroft's funeral, our nieces' baptisms and a few Christmas masses. Not till your sister got him going again."

"He told me."

"Kevin?"

Megan finished her glass. "Don't sound so shocked. He took me for a walk this morning. We started with the bogs. I saw Drew and Holly's house on the hill and I had a tour of the house where all of you grew up.

"He mentioned you'd been out."

"Erin's turning your bedroom into the nursery."

"So I understand."

"He had a lot to say, Jody, about Erin and his life. He told me that Holly, Anne and Sky had their weddings in their own churches but it was Erin's idea to be married here, the way your parents were."

"Erin never told you that?"

"I'm not sure I ever gave her the chance, or maybe she assumed I didn't want to hear it."

"Be flattered that Kevin told you. If he opened up to you, it was for Erin's sake. It's no secret you've been something of a threat."

"Family above all else."

"Out of necessity all those years."

She grew pensive, but there was mischief in her eyes. "I told him he was a man of few words, and he said he left the words to the attorney in the family."

Megan looked through the panes and her breath frosted the antique glass. "I'm not sure they come much easier to you, Jody, unless you're solving somebody else's problems."

Jody stood next to her, wrapped in her presence. He took a deep breath and let her fragrance intoxicate him. She'd walked the bogs, toured his house, discussed him with Kevin. His nerves were on fire. He needed another walk, alone over a dark field. He cleared his throat.

She was still looking out at the church. "He told me about Peter finding you over there, when you were nine, yelling at God for making your life different."

Kevin? "What third grader wants to be different? Every other kid had a mother who baked cupcakes on his birthday and brought them to class."

"Except you," Megan replied. "Peter brought in a pizza with nine candles in it."

Jody looked at her. She was searching his face for a hint of what he was feeling. "And when I complained, Kevin yanked me behind the barn and threatened me with foster care if I became a behavior problem. I hitchhiked into town and hid in the church. Kevin seems to have told you all about it."

"You never rebelled again."

"Drew and Ryan had that market cornered. I would have sent Peter and Kevin over the edge if I'd followed in their footsteps."

Megan looked curious. "Do I detect a note of sarcasm?"

"From me, the model Branigan?"

"Now there's an accurate assessment. Governor Branigan was mentioned again."

"Just how long did you two talk?"

"Long enough for me to look at things a little differently."

"What things?"

"I've told you, my sister's future in your family for one."

"And for another?"

"Your place in it, too. Your reticence."

Her eyes were bright, as enticing as the drape of yellow silk clinging to her, enticing beyond endurance, nearly. Her smile became enigmatic.

He tried to joke. "A little knowledge is a dangerous thing."

"It's only fair. You've been looking at me through Erin's eyes and now I get to see you through Kevin's. I like what I see, Counselor."

Megan's deep throaty laugh dissolved the last of his resolve. He put down his glass and took her by the hand, surprised and encouraged when she didn't resist. They crossed the foyer and went into the empty library.

Impulsively he pushed his fingers through her hair and gently tilted her head. Her eyes were dreamy, heavy lidded, and she parted her lips.

"We'll be missed, Jody. Make it quick," she said with a catch in her voice.

He paused and bent to her ear. "No, Megan, soon, when we won't be missed, we'll make it last all night."

"Why, Jody Branigan! That's why you dragged me in here?"

"Yes," he muttered.

"I hardly know you."

"Megan O'Connor, it may not have been long, but you know me better than any other woman on earth does."

Fifteen

Her eyes widened. "I believe that. The only way to get into that head of yours is to poke around your family. The curious thing is, Jody, maybe I know you better than you know yourself. Since fate has dropped me so unceremoniously at your feet, I might just take your brother up on his suggestion. It might take some of the misery out of my circumstances."

"What suggestion?" rolled from the back of his constricted throat.

"He thought getting to know you might be worth the effort. Erin's mentioned it, as well. For some time, actually." She stared again, seriously, mischievously. "Do you have any idea how your green eyes darken when you're passionate? They're a barometer to your feelings, not that you're doing much to hide them."

He closed his eyes and rested his cheek against hers. "This time last week I was kissing you in your cow pasture."

Stirred by his breath in her ear, Megan tensed and Jody felt her palm flatten over his chest.

Jody ran his index finger down her spine, skimming over the neat row of tiny buttons that fastened her dress. She arched her back, torturing him with the whispered laugh he adored, then slid her hand around to his back and stepped forward until her breasts grazed his chest. The moment he closed his arms around her, she shuddered.

"Has it only been that long since I found you stretched out on that hotel bed in nearly nothing?"

"Megan!"

She leaned against him and matched his breathing. "There's such comfort in this, Jody. In two weeks I'll be moving to Millbrook. Will I be able to count on you?"

"You have to ask?"

"It's going to be tough at first."

"I'm here, for just about anything."

"Wicked!" She put her weight fully on her feet. The mischief was gone from her eyes. "We need to talk."

"We are."

"I am. You're not."

Jody looked at the empty door frame. "Megan, this isn't necessary."

"Of course it is. You and I are sprinting in one direction." She waved at the air. "Call it what you want, Jody, but keep a clear head. It's important for you and for me."

He groaned. "Don't you know what the sound of your voice does to my circulatory system, even when you're reading me the Riot Act? Don't speak like that here.''

"Then where, the front seat of your car with your hands roaming and me tearing at your shirt buttons?''

"All right, all right." He forced himself to reply.

"The point I want to make is that I need your friendship. I need it much more than the other stuff.'' Again she waved dismissively. "I'd like to be able to depend on you.''

"You can, Megan. Of course you can.''

"This—pull—we're feeling is probably temporary. It'll evaporate if we give it time, but I need you now, even while it's in the way.''

Knots, that's what the woman was doing, tying him in emotional knots. She needed him *in spite of* what they felt for each other. He wanted to ask what exactly she had, or didn't have in mind, but he was not at all sure he wanted to hear her answer.

"You can count on me, Megan, complicated or simple." He hoped he'd covered all his bases.

The sound of voices came from the parlor across the hall and someone laughed in the dining room. With reluctance, Jody put her at arm's length. "There's more here than friendship."

"But that's where we should start. I'm not one to start at the finish line.''

"Did you have in mind a fifty-yard dash or a marathon?''

Megan came forward and kissed him fully on the mouth. "I can't say, but I understand pacing is everything.''

After the supper, Erin tossed her bouquet from the staircase and it was caught by Sean's youngster Katy, thanks to a sudden boost in the air from her father. The bride looked down at her sisters and winked.

She and Kevin left for their abbreviated honeymoon amidst more hugs, kisses and tears on the lawn. Jody stood with his hands in his pockets and watched until his brother's Corvette disappeared around the bend in the road.

"I happen to have a free evening," came wafting at his ear.

Jody turned to find Megan rubbing the chill from her arms. The feel of her lips still burned in his memory and he surprised himself by shaking his head. "Being alone with you plays havoc with my blood pressure. I'll stay, but it'll be right here, unless you've changed your mind about a fifty-yard dash. I want Hugh, Bridget, Ryan, Sky and Matt in the same room with us."

She took his arm and they followed the others. "Afraid of a little honest conversation?"

"Among other things."

"Such flattery."

There was not so much as another kiss. Jody stayed, enjoyed all the O'Connor company and said a chaste good-night and farewell just after midnight. She walked him out to his car.

"I have another favor to ask," she said.

"Try me."

"Don't call me. I'll be back in two weeks and in the meantime, I'd like to try and make some sense of this."

"I've had a bit of difficulty with that, myself."

She laughed and Jody was left with the memory of it as he drove away.

In the two weeks until Megan returned for her six-month stint, he might do well to follow her lead. His head could use some clearing, as well.

Promises under the influence of passion were easily made and in the cool air of the spring nights that followed, doubt crept in. It had nothing to do with his desire for her. Jody's responsibilities to his firm and his clients, coupled with those to the bogs consumed most of his waking hours.

"Magnanimous gestures," he muttered to himself. Jody didn't take women strolling through the Branigan homestead or over the bogs. He didn't engage them in long family discussions. There was never time or need for platonic friendships. He had women business associates, he had sisters-in-law, he had the occasional date and he had work. Reluctantly, he admitted during the cold drive home that he didn't have women friends.

He didn't know what Megan expected, or even if he were capable of living up to those expectations. Life had let her down temporarily. What if he made it worse? What if he couldn't be what she wanted? A net of entanglements, the very things he'd sworn to avoid, had somehow been lowered right down over him. Somehow!

She had the acumen of a trial lawyer and the perception of a grand jury, yet she insisted that she needed him. How could she be so self-assured and directed one minute and so lost the next? And how, damn it all, did she manage to get right into his soul every time she focused those blue eyes on him?

Jody drew on every ounce of professionalism he possessed and put Megan on the back burner, where the thought of her return continued to simmer. He

spent the first part of the week in Boston on behalf of
the Lobstermen's Association, which left only nights
at home to prepare for Drew and Holly's hearing before the Conservation Commission.

The family overtime exhausted him, but it was where
his interest lay and three nights in a row, unable to
sleep, he worked at his desk till two in the morning. He
accompanied Holly and Drew to the hearing and presented the case for opening the Taft property. As he
had suspected, the Commission held back on a decision, extending the final determination to the next
meeting.

Saturday Kevin and Erin returned, jubilant, from
Palm Beach. Jody went out to the homestead for a
welcome home drink and stayed long enough to discuss the problems facing the Taft project.

Kevin walked him back out to his car when they'd
finished. "I know what this has done to your free
time."

"I'll be damned if I remember what that is."

Kevin smiled. "When Megan arrives, I hope she'll
remind you."

Jody leaned against his car. "Look, Big Brother—"

"It's only a suggestion. You could use a little diver-
sion."

"Your idea or your wife's?"

"Megan's, if I know women."

Jody's heart jumped but he scoffed. "Not a prayer."

Jody spent Sunday morning alone at the marina with
his boat, and his thoughts. The fiery redhead consumed much of his contemplation. There was nothing
between them but a bunch of sparks and already he was
under the Branigan microscope. For the first time, he

suffered pangs for what the rest of them had gone through. The rest of them...the bogs...the pump house. Even Megan couldn't keep back the mental hashing and rehashing of his career.

That night the wind was down and he drove out to the bogs. The temperature still dropped when the sun set and all-night vigils during the odd frost warnings were commonplace for his brothers. Even in spring, the occasional frost required the bogs to be sprayed all night from their underground sprinkler systems. Though it was not as critical as fall frost, which could kill the ripe berries and wipe out an entire crop overnight, it was still imperative that the budding spring vines be monitored carefully. Many a night any or all of his brothers were out.

It added to his fatigue, but was something Jody, too, wanted to stay part of. Unlike Kevin, Drew or Ryan, he had no system to alert him to frost warnings except the weather reports. Boston television had predicted a dip into the high thirties and so he drove into Millbrook. His brothers would be out, scattered over their property. The time had come to talk.

Sixteen

───

Jody's headlights caught the spray from the sprinkler system as he pulled up next to Drew's pickup truck. He and Ryan were at the dike and Kevin was shining his flashlight over the pump house.

"Don't you get enough of the cranberry business from the paperwork we bury you under?" Ryan asked as his brother strolled over.

"Couldn't sleep."

"Jody, we didn't send you to law school so you could stay up all night checking sprinkler heads," Drew threw in.

"I want to be here, all right?"

"Suit yourself. It's a good place to think, even for lawyers, I guess." Drew went out ahead of them.

"I guess," Jody muttered.

Ryan was grinning. "Good place for other things, too. You'll have to line up some midnight monitoring with Megan when she gets back. Best thing in the world for romance: cold nights, wide open spaces, a woman too good to resist . . ."

"What gave you the impression I can't resist Megan?"

"What'd I say?"

"Forget it. I'm on edge, that's all."

"No kidding."

"Don't put Megan in the same category as Sky."

"Sky, Holly, Erin, and Anne all got moonstruck out here."

"One moonstruck O'Connor is enough for the family," he muttered and walked into the darkness along the dike.

"Jody—"

"Drop it, Ryan."

The older brother fell silent, but he caught up and matched Jody's pace.

"Sorry," Jody mumbled.

"Forget it. I know Megan's a sore subject. I shouldn't have needled you," he replied as Drew and Kevin returned. He ran the beam of his flashlight over the ditch and stooped to inspect a vine. "What else has you so stressed out?"

Jody looked down at Ryan and then at the other two. "Life."

"Tell me about it," Drew answered. "We've got another baby coming, Holly wants to start her MBA and if the reclamation project gets approval, we've got thirty percent more productivity to deal with."

"Want me to throw in the bank loan for the sprinklers, replacement of the pump house and impending parenthood?" Kevin added.

"This isn't some damn joke, Kevin."

Ryan turned the beam on Jody. "What's eating you? I didn't think bachelor Porsche owners with thriving careers and money to burn knew the meaning of *stress*."

Jody shoved his hands in his pockets. They were clammy and his heart was racing. He looked at them, Drew the only easy-going Branigan, Ryan and Kevin, the most volatile. He listened to himself say, "I want out."

Drew nodded. "I can't blame you. There's no good reason why you should be here in the middle of the night monitoring with us. That's your doing, kid. You could use the sleep."

Ryan added, "You're right about the rest of it, though. We've piled all the legal stuff on your shoulders." He shrugged an apology.

"If it's too much, I can get somebody else to review the Pest project. There's no crime in admitting there's too much to carry," Kevin said.

Jody's heart was in his throat. They had it backwards, all three of them. Three of them . . . Sean made four. He looked at the shadowed figures of his brothers. Would working out here day after day swamp him in family? Was it just another set of problems with which to cope? Could he cope?

His head ached. Maybe the appeal of the bogs lay in the distance, the longing for what he thought he couldn't have. He took a deep breath. His chest hurt.

"It's not too much," he managed to reply. "I'm just strung out, that's all. I'll be fine." He pressed his breastbone.

"Jody." The sound of his name was accompanied by the touch of Ryan's hand on his shoulder.

"I'll be fine." He took the flashlight from his brother's hand and marched along the dike to see for himself that the sprinkler heads were clear, all the while feeling their concern like a blanket draped on his shoulders. Ryan, Drew and Kevin let him go.

Though they could have used his help, Jody left under his brothers' insistence. Back on Saquish Street, he threw back some painkillers and stripped down to his shorts. In the dark, stretched across his bed, he pressed his chest and ignored the pain.

What did he want? After all they'd done, why couldn't he just be content? His career was taking off. After all the years of hard work, he was finally being rewarded for the effort. He could even pay them back.

The monologue did nothing but increase his headache and after punching his pillow into shape, he flung his arm out and waited for sleep. As always, it was slow in coming and as Jody lay there, he moved his hand across the mattress. He felt the sheet and the contours of the empty pillow with the same hand that had cupped Megan's breast and felt her heart, Megan's heart. It had pounded against his and, under him, she had seemed to mold into every hollow.

"Megan," he said to the darkness, as if saying it would keep the emptiness from swallowing him.

Seventeen

Friday night the Conservation Commission reconvened in a special session called to discuss the Taft project. When Jody stood before them for the second time, he had Drew by his side. It was the first of any Branigans Jody had seen since the midnight tongue-lashing, but they both were concentrating on the immediate business.

The committee handed down its decision. The members took the unprecedented step of requiring a groundwater survey before it would allow the Branigans to expand, explaining that their first consideration was maintaining clean drinking water.

Jody advised Drew to request a ruling from the Appeals Board in hopes that they could at least proceed with maintenance on the existing bogs. When it was over, he walked with his brother through the dark parking lot of Town Hall, talking business.

Drew sighed. "At least you can stick all this back in your briefcase while we sweat out the wait. It's not the first time I've wished I were the lawyer, drawing a salary from something a little more secure than agriculture."

Jody was sardonic. "Maybe we ought to trade professions."

"Tough it out, Jody. Times get bad for all of us. You had us all worried that night at the bogs."

He was too tired and the moment was wrong. Jody didn't respond. They separated and Jody returned to Plymouth over the dark back roads. The bogs lay flat and black on either side of him. He left them behind and entered Plymouth, bright under the street lamps, but equally quiet. Though he was exhausted, instead of heading up Saquish Street, he parked at the harbor.

At the end of the town pier, a single light shone in the harbormaster's office and the draggers and lobster boats swayed on their moorings. His catboat would be launched soon. For the second year in a row, because of his work load, he'd hired the marina to varnish it. Though he enjoyed the labor and the camaraderie of the yard, there hadn't been time to do it himself.

Jody pulled his tie loose and unbuttoned the top of his starched dress shirt, then sat on the granite seawall. The air smelled of working boats, seafood restaurants and tidal flats. Above him a gull screeched under a moon grown full since he'd walked beneath it at Valley View, the same moon shining down on Megan's last night in New Jersey. The bird swooped and settled on the peak of the harbormaster's office. How bloody easy to be a sea gull and do nothing but follow the draggers from first light till dusk. The night air was biting but he stayed until he was nearly numb, then went back to the still-warm Porsche and headed for bed.

Hours later, in the dark he awoke with a start. Jody lay still, pulse racing, and listened: he heard nothing; the house was quiet. He turned and focused on the glow of the bedside clock. It was nearly 1:00 a.m.; there were hours left till morning. As he rolled over, the doorbell sounded from the living room, in one drawn-out buzz.

Alarm brought him fully awake. There was no sense in calling out. The front door was down a flight of stairs. Instead he pulled a terry-cloth robe over his boxer shorts and hurried through the living room, tying it as he went.

Family would call...fellow tenants would have come up the stairs...the police...his car...had there been sirens? He went downstairs barefoot, rubbed his hand over his eyes and looked through the sidelights of the front door, still trying to calm his respiratory system.

Under the porch light, Megan O'Connor was leaning against a support pillar, looking out into the street. She had one hand holding back her hair, and jeans worn to the softness of suede clung to her. They were faded to the blue of her eyes and a patch of her calf peeked from a hole just below the back of her knee. She had on two plaid oversized flannel shirts and rag-tag boat shoes. The effect and the contrast, after memories of linen suits, silk dresses and high heels, was mesmerizing.

At the sound of his throwing the latch, she turned around and beamed. As he swung open the door, she waved with such an expression of relief and happiness that arousal drained the blood from the rest of his body. His chest was tight and his heart sounded a new alarm.

"I'm here," she said as she stepped closer. "Early."

He tried to remain civilized. "Very," he managed. "Come in."

"I changed my plans. I rented that small trailer over there and had a hitch put on the car." She pointed across the street and then crossed the threshold and followed him up the stairs. "There wasn't a lot to bring, since Erin left so much. What I didn't need, Dad took back to Valley View," her voice came from behind him as they climbed the stairs. Jody led the way into his living room and snapped on a single lamp.

She punched his arm lightly. "I drove right over the George Washington Bridge with all the truckers. It wasn't bad. Night's the perfect time to travel, actually. Lighter traffic but everything's still open on the interstates." Her smile danced. "In the morning I'll need a friend with a strong back."

Jody rubbed his jaw. "Does anyone know you've arrived?"

"It's so late I didn't want to just pull up to the carriage house and wake up the Morgans. I was going to go to Erin and Kevin's—"

"I'm glad you didn't."

They stood facing each other in the dim light. Megan sighed in obvious relief. "I'm glad you said that."

"Megan?" He was drowning in the husky tremor clouding her voice, belying her words. Her eyes were wide, bright, but full of doubt.

"No one's expecting me till tomorrow. All the way up here I kept thinking that you might have changed your mind about helping, that I'm just one more obligation and you have so many. You didn't call—"

"You asked me not to. It was a stupid request. There must have been a hundred times I wanted to talk with you."

"You, too? I nearly called so many times. It was tempting."

"Do you ever give in to temptation?"

"I'm here, Jody," she whispered.

"Tell me why," he whispered back.

"To make sure whatever this is between us wasn't just my imagination."

Jody pulled her to him. It was as if only hours, not weeks, had passed. The old rhythm, the repartee were immediate. Her mood swing was his undoing. It cloaked his still rampant desire in an equally masculine and primal emotion: protection. She needed him and her need was salve to his own. Megan O'Connor was the only person in his universe capable of making him live for the moment.

"It feels awfully real to me," he murmured at her temple. The sound of his name was muffled along the side of his neck, on his cheek, and then he crushed her mouth with his.

He was too rough, he was too fast, the caution light flashed in his head, but Megan clung to him, matching the hunger.

He held her face and reveled in the taste of her. "This is crazy."

"I know," she gasped, but her response was an urgency impossible to miss. "It's just chemistry."

Jody groaned, not caring what it was. She kept one hand deep in his hair almost chastely, the other at the nape of his neck as she welcomed his kisses.

"Counselor, my whole life is crazy. I've had so much to think about, to worry over and all I see when I close my eyes is you. Days and days of nothing but Jody Branigan dead to the world, wearing a skimpy pair of boxer shorts and a half-smile from some sexy dream."

"The dream was opening my eyes and finding you at the foot of the bed." He kissed her again and the tide rushed in him, a moon-tide he ached to drown in. "Come to this bed, Megan."

"Even if it's just for the moment?"

"Here and now is a good place to start. Let me make love to you." In the inches between them he caressed the flannel of her shirts and drifted over the contours, front and back. Megan moaned and he kissed the hollow of her throat, feeling her pulse pound against his mouth. Deftly he worked the long row of her shirt buttons, until they were all undone. He bent lower and kissed the rise of her soft flesh.

Megan arched her back and gasped. Even the catch of her voice made his blood surge. He closed his eyes to steady himself and she captured his tongue with hers. Abruptly, the touch of her hands disappeared. Still, they kissed and, without looking, he lifted his hands to her shoulders and slid her shirts down her arms, dropping them at her feet. When he cupped her lace-covered breasts, explosions of pleasure tightened every muscle in his body. "It's been a long time since anything felt this right," he whispered. "God, I love looking at you."

She gently pressed her warm hands to his face. "What do you see?"

"Desire, Megan, even in this light, maybe as strong as mine. Don't try to hide it."

"It's too late for that." She rained kisses along his jaw, then returned to his mouth. He heard the soft purr in her throat and her silky plunder drove the tide higher.

He couldn't stand much more. The only thing stronger than his ache for release was his will to make the moment last. Touching her drove the pain and frustration of the world away. As long as Megan was in his arms, anything was bearable.

"Touch me," Jody whispered as he pulled her denim covered hips close.

"Yes." Megan slid her hands under his robe. They were trembling.

"It's wonderful; you're beautiful," he told her as she continued. She mimicked him by kissing the hollow of his throat, his muscled chest and the spot over his pounding heart. There was such heat in her touch, he moaned.

"Heaven," she murmured.

"Come closer." He swayed against her hips, and the contrast of denim with the rough terry of his robe made the heat beneath nearly unbearable. Megan's magic tore through him, forced into every crevice of his hardened body with a speed that took his breath away. His hands spread across the soft, worn seat of her jeans and pressed her to him as if she would vanish if he were to let go.

Her cheeks were flushed with passion and her eyes were bright. "Show me, Jody," she whispered.

He covered her hands. "I'd love to."

She kissed his knuckles.

"How are you at untying knots," he asked as he pushed her hands roughly toward his robe sash.

She pretended to fumble. "This may take some time."

He closed his eyes and the first touch of her fingers made him catch his breath. There was desperation in his laugh.

"I may have to work at this," she murmured as she brushed his skin.

"God, Megan, hurry!"

She didn't. Instead, she inched her way along, deepening the torment until every muscle in his body was as tight as piano wire. Nothing else had ever felt this good. The sash fell away and she opened his robe. Megan kissed his shoulder and slipped the robe off as he'd done with her shirts. She put her face next to his. "I'm copying you," she said in his ear. As if to prove it, she cupped his hips, then slid her hands over the cotton of his shorts and around to the back. She swayed against the sweet torture of his arousal until he was nearly beyond standing.

"Let's even things up," he managed as he unfastened the brass button, then spread the zipper of her jeans. He could feel the ebb of her own self-control as he pushed them down her long legs.

"There's nothing left in my knees, Jody," she groaned.

His laugh was still husky. "Then we'd better lie down."

She put her arms around his neck and he picked her up. As he carried her into the bedroom, she pressed her palm over his heart and her cheek against his. "I've felt your heart thundering. Mine has matched it, Jody, beat for beat since that first afternoon."

In reply, he laid her on the bed. The room was washed only in the gold lamplight from the next room and gray moonlight from the window. They eased each other from the bits of clothing left and he could just make out the rapture in Megan's expression as he settled next to her and traced the lines of her body.

Never still, she caressed him, beginning with his scalp, his jaw and the planes of his face, kissing his blazing skin, inch by inch, wherever her fingers had been.

"Jody," she said breathlessly as her fingertips raced down his spine, "oh, Jody, even back in that hotel room I thought about this."

From head to waist, she ignited him. Her touch seared him. She skimmed across his scalp, his shoulders and chest, down to the base of his backbone until his head swam with the wash of his own pulse.

With what minimal self-control remained, he grabbed her wrist. "Wait," he gasped and stopped just long enough to scramble through his top drawer for protection. As he turned back, Megan opened her arms. Her body had taken on an incredible softness, heightened by shadows. He ached to melt into her and blend with the half light until he was in sweet oblivion. Had she been anyone else, he would have done just that.

"Jody?"

"Not yet. Savor it with me, Megan. God, you're beautiful in the moonlight," he managed.

She looked up at him. "And tomorrow, when you're struggling with my furniture, I want to remember how gorgeous *you* are in nothing but shadows." She slid her hand along his chest. "I want to remember how you *felt* in nothing but shadows."

Happiness danced in her face. He kissed her and then began a slow, incredible journey over her, lingering on the fullness of her breasts until she arched against him. Over the thundering of his own pulse in his ears he heard "Jody!" again and again. Her nipples swelled and tightened under his kisses and then he moved to the flat plain of her stomach.

"Now, Jody, now," she cried.

He balanced over her and brushed back her hair. He'd meant to wait, to be sure, at last, that her fulfillment would be as complete as his. There was no more waiting. He looked down, into her wide blue eyes as she clung to him. Her touch was sudden, white hot and rough along the inside of his thigh. He lost all power to concentrate on anything except the feel of her underneath him.

Jody plunged into her and the simplest movement drowned him in sensations. Their names mingled in the dark. Megan's rushed rhythm slowed; Jody's quickened until the match was perfect. Like a swell at sea, ecstasy built in him as Megan's passion engulfed her, rolling and breaking only to build again. His own rose, crested and with a cry, he joined her in the floodtide of rapture.

They lay still, panting, returning as slowly as they could to reality.

"Do I hear a sea gull?" she asked softly, finally.

"Probably."

"Jody—"

He touched her lips. "Don't talk. I'm being very selfish." He pulled her against him, burying his face in her tumbled hair. "You give me this incredible sense of peace, Megan. Stay with me tonight."

Megan was on her side, tracing his shoulder with her index finger. "Tonight. Only because no one's expecting me. The last thing either of us needs is to be under the scrutiny of our families."

"Any more than we already are."

"Mmm."

A million bits of conversation drifted through him but he wasn't about to shatter the mood. Instead, he tucked her up against his chest and fell asleep.

Eighteen

Saturday morning filtered through the sugar maple outside the window and splayed sunlight over the rumpled bed covers. Megan stirred and Jody woke as she slid her hand over his chest. He pulled her into the crook of his arm as peace renewed itself.

"Good morning," he said.

"Hi."

"Any regrets, now that you're here?"

She came up on one elbow. "Regrets?"

"About the transfer."

"Too soon to tell."

"About last night?"

"None. And you, Jody?"

He smiled. "First good night's sleep I've had in ages."

Megan shifted until she'd stretched out over him. "Got your mind off your worries, I guess."

Afraid she might move, he ran his hands down her spine and over the sweet rise of her bottom. "I guess!"

"How've things been these two weeks? Start with the Taft project."

He tried, but she rose on her elbow to look at him and her breasts molded against his chest. Under the flat plain of her stomach, he stirred.

She kissed him. "Not yet. Talk to me. Business before pleasure."

He talked. Cradled to him like a second skin, Megan listened and remarked. She coaxed when she had to, though he was barely aware of it and his words spilled the way his heart had.

Finally, in midsentence Megan moaned. He brushed his hands down along her thighs and felt the magic begin again. "Enough business?"

"This feels too good to be business."

"Then it must be pleasure," he said.

"Incredible chemistry," she whispered as she shuddered against him.

"Incredible." Jody reached again for protection, then lay on his back.

Under the sheets, Megan began to caress him. Her hands were everywhere and this time the heat from her touch was intensified tenfold by memory. Impatiently Jody kicked at the bed covers.

She caught the quilt and he covered her wrist. "Don't hide. Look at me, Megan. Let me look at you."

Color mottled her cheeks. "Somehow, in the moonlight—"

He ran his thumb over her collarbone. "Remembering you in the moonlight is what makes me want to see you now."

She smiled shyly. "All right."

He stayed on his back. "Push the covers down."

She leaned over and traced the curve of his mouth with her tongue as she slowly lowered the quilt from her breasts. Desire danced over him. Megan shifted. She knelt and pushed the rumpled covers further, beyond his feet. The ache in him deepened.

Sunlight played over her where shadows had been the night before. A yellow band undulated over her shoulder blades and spine as she pushed the covers to the foot of the bed. From the pillow, Jody watched her turn around. Megan's smile was laced with passion and her breasts swayed in the sunbeam.

"Come here."

He reached up and put his hands on her shoulders, expecting her to lie down beside him. Instead she stayed on her knees and leaned over, opening her hands over his chest. The sound of her soft, deep breathing made his blood surge.

He entwined one hand in her hair and pulled her down until he could rain kisses where the sun had been. His palms tingled with the feel of her skin. "So smooth and soft," he sighed, closing his eyes.

"Rough and firm," she replied, gliding her hand over him. "All I can think about is last night."

"Show me."

He sat up. Her hands trembled as she caressed, lightly, until his pleasure was palpable. "Megan," he cried and within moments, every touch was rhythmic and deliberate. He groaned her name and looked hard into her eyes. Passion had darkened them to slate, deep as the bay, dreamy. Her skin flamed when he touched her, and quickly, roughly, he traced the stain from her cheeks, down along her jaw, her neck, to her breasts. "Beautiful," he murmured.

The soft weight warmed in his palms. As he circled her nipples with his thumbs, she arched back. His name caught in her throat and it drove him to the edge of something he'd never experienced.

"Please, Jody—"

None of it was enough. "Now, Megan." He sank back into the pillow and grasped her hips, guiding her. She twisted, then arrow straight, she found him. There was no relief, only incredible need to join with Megan. He'd never known such hunger.

With a cry she lowered herself slowly over every inch of him. The magic was rough and instant. As she clung to him, Jody led her through a maze of pleasure. With every thrust, her rapture intensified his. She filled his head as he filled her body. The peak engulfed them and waves of ecstasy replaced the hunger, soldering their spirits.

For long, peace-filled moments, Jody lay with Megan in his arms. When they finally got out of bed, the sun was above the trees.

Jody pulled on jeans and a heavy sweater over his turtleneck as Megan got back into her flannel shirts and denim. He bought her breakfast at the corner deli and they walked to the boat yard with coffee, talking of public service projects, communications, sailing and family.

The air was cool and the stiff, unsettled breeze was typical for early May. *Respite* was up on jacks with a ladder against her transom, the bright blue tarp pulled back to reveal a superb varnish job on the teak trim. Jody climbed aboard and gave Megan a hand. Around them any number of colorful sea dogs were making repairs and putting last-minute shines on their vessels. Jody watched Megan as she glanced at a lobsterman tinkering with his engine. He smiled when she turned back and admired his own boat's bright work and the beamy lines. Fiberglass seats lined the cockpit and he motioned her to sit down.

"There'll be cushions out here, of course."

She glanced from bow to stern. "And a mast and tiller, I assume."

"Soon. The yard's launching her this week." They drank their coffee and let the salt air cool them off.

Megan put her face to the air. "It smells as distinctive as the farm, doesn't it."

"Sea bottom and fish, salt air and diesel fuel."

"Do you belong to a yacht club?"

"I'd thought you would have checked my credentials long ago."

Megan winced, then looked out at the yard and the gray shapes of pleasure boats still under their protective tarpaulins. "Idle curiosity, that's all. A man who drives a Porsche and does business on Wall Street might belong to a yacht club. I really don't care about your credentials."

Though he knew otherwise, he let it pass. "Matt and I are members of the Saquish Yacht Club where we have a slip. I'm fronting Matt's dues until he starts earning some money. Through the law firm I'm also a member of the Commonwealth Club in Boston and primarily for business reasons, I've joined the Millbrook Country Club. In my next life I hope I'll have time for tennis or golf.

"I'm a season subscriber to the Plymouth Philharmonic Orchestra and as a family we underwrite one performance a year. We also support the Women's Services program at the medical clinic. I forgot the Red Sox. We have season passes to Fenway Park, too."

"Erin's already told me most of that." She shook her finger at him. "You're making fun of me."

"No, a woman should know who she's involved with."

Megan leaned back against the hard coaming. "We are involved, aren't we?"

"Yes." The sun was sharp and Jody cupped her face. "You're looking for answers but I'm not sure you're asking the right questions."

"As in, 'Where do we go from here?' I didn't mean to get involved with you, with anyone. I didn't have any intention of this happening."

"Surprised me, too."

"I know. I find that oddly comforting. You seem as disconcerted as I feel. I'm not like Erin, Jody. I'm sure you see that."

"I see that you're more cautious, more sophisticated. You're not as crazy about the Holsteins in your background as she is."

She stared into her coffee for an inordinate amount of time before looking up at him.

Jody palmed his cup. "That's quite a look you're giving me."

"My head's spinning from all this."

"That's it?"

"That's it? I feel like I'm living someone else's life. I've moved hundreds of miles to a strange town, taken on a new job and fallen in love." Sharply, she looked up at him.

"Have you?"

"Yes, I think I have."

"I was willing to take it for simple chemistry, pull, initial rush. Any other terms of yours I've missed?"

"How can you joke when I'm on the verge of an anxiety attack? *Everything* is happening too fast. We had no business making love . . . twice!" The last was a mutter.

"A complete breach of decorum."

She scowled. "A complete lapse of sanity."

"I thought you needed me."

She sighed and took a gulp of her coffee. "I do. I need a friend, Jody. I need some support while I get acclimated. What I don't need—"

He bent forward and kissed her. "I spent all night thinking I'm irresistible. Don't spoil it."

"That's the trouble, Counselor. You are." Megan drained her cup.

"Megan, you make me forget there's anything else in my life but the feel of you in my arms. You can't begin to know how important that's becoming."

"Stop right there. I can't afford to be that important, not with my own life so shaken up."

"You'll be settled before you know it. In a week, all this will be routine. Kevin'll have you out there cleaning ditches in no time."

"I'm not the cleaning ditches type."

Jody considered the dregs in his cup and gave her a slow smile. When he knew he could get away with it, he reached over and burrowed his fingers beneath the open throat of her shirts. He stopped with his fingers pressing the steady heartbeat beneath the soft swell of her breast. Megan immediately covered his hand with hers. "Still thundering, Counselor."

"Since the very first moment, back in my hotel room."

"Joke if you have to. This isn't funny."

"Why isn't it? A man and woman fall madly in love, sister of the woman doesn't approve, brother of the man is sent to straighten her out and boom, first thing you know—"

"Don't finish that!"

"All right, I'll change tack. Does it help that I'm not much like Kevin?" He moved his hand and sat back.

"No. If you were like Kevin or the others, this wouldn't have happened in the first place. You're a lawyer, you're educated, you're cosmopolitan."

"I ride in limousines and have business in New York. I drive a fancy car and keep a boat in the harbor. None of this would have happened if I simply grew cranberries for a living?"

"To be honest, probably not."

That caught him like a sharp blow, but he let her continue.

"I never felt a thing for the boys growing up around me, the ones with their futures all mapped out on their family farms. You're an enigma, Jody. It's all so confusing and fascinating. You're much too appealing for your own good." She looked at him without humor before shifting and pushing her hair away from her temple. "What if I fall in love with Millbrook, but you and I don't work? What if I get transferred again or lose my job?"

Jody played with her hair. "I thought you were only interested in tomorrow."

"I was. I am. Complications give me migraines. How can you be so casual about it?"

"Because none of it has happened."

"But it might."

"It's a risk." He kissed her then, to keep down the worry.

The moment they stopped, Megan pressed her cheek against his. "I don't want to be responsible for your heart, Jody, and I don't want you responsible for mine."

"It's too late. You know it as well as I do."

She kissed him then. "How did this happen?"

"Megs, another month around the Branigans and you won't have to ask."

They walked back to Saquish Street and Megan went directly to her car. "If you breathe a word of this to anyone—"

He waved the comment away. "I'll come by in a while. You get started unpacking. Go pound on Ryan's door. Pretend you've just arrived if that's so important."

"It is and I will. You look rested, Jody."

"You're better than warm milk. I'll be out in an hour or two. I have some work to do first."

"There's always more work."

He nodded.

His response obviously troubled her. "You're restless, Jody. I saw it in New York and out at the farm. Back then I thought it was being away from home, the stress of Wall Street, but it's still with you."

He shrugged. "I've got a lot on my mind."

"You're great at straightening out other people's lives, knowing what's good for them. Take care of your own. Follow Kevin's advice and leave the bogs to your brothers."

He opened her car door.

Megan had the audacity to smile and kissed him, hard, full on the mouth until he was breathless with surprise and renewed desire. "You're a magnificent-looking man, but I'm just as interested in this." She tapped his forehead. "Megan O'Connor in your life is a package deal. Where her body goes, her brain follows. I would expect the same from you."

"You drive a hard bargain."

"You're the one who's been so glib about risk. I don't want your heart, Jody, if you can't trust me with your feelings. You're hell-bent on putting my life back together and I'm enjoying it. However, it's beginning to dawn on me that all this concentration on my life keeps you from thinking about yours. Something's responsible for those headaches I'm not supposed to know you get. Give that some thought.''

Megan stopped the lecture, assured him she knew the way back to Millbrook and got into her car. As an afterthought, she rolled down her window. ''Whatever this is between us—''

''Is just between us,'' he finished for her. Neither wanted it any other way.

Jody waved her off and stayed in the street watching the brake lights on her trailer until the car disappeared around the corner at the bottom of the hill. When Megan was out of sight, he shoved his hands in his pockets and went to the house.

Nineteen

Who was he to blithely assure her that involvement was worth the risk of heartbreak? He was no more sure of anything than Megan, and had nothing more to go on than the invisible, improbable pull that held her to him.

She was right that he had some thinking to do. A clean break from Megan would never be possible. She was family and a transfer to Outer Mongolia wouldn't change it. Compared to her life, his was as rough as the harbor during a nor'easter and it was a storm he rode alone.

As if that weren't enough, all the elements in his life she found so appealing were what shackled him to his self-doubts. He knew his own heart; his career was killing him. He also knew that if he were to tell her that he wanted to grow cranberries, that he intended to convince Kevin . . . what he had with Megan, what she called love, would shrivel like last year's vines.

Megan moved in. In true Branigan fashion, Jody's brothers and their wives involved themselves in every detail. They lifted, carried, unpacked, fed, advised and welcomed her. She was cordial at first, warming up to all of them as the week progressed. She accepted her surroundings and took WJQG to heart, sharing her excitement about the public affairs schedule with any Branigans who happened to be her host and hostess that evening.

In the days that followed, Megan settled into her job and her new life with increasing enthusiasm. Jody settled into a perpetual state of arousal. His body took on a life of its own, kicking into a high gear he hadn't known existed. Megan's voice, which had never failed to stir him, was now the texture of honey.

It seemed heavy with unconscious intimacy when she spoke to him on the phone or ordered lunch, when he found time to take her. To spare themselves family speculation, they went to absurd lengths to appear no more than friendly in-laws and he never so much as drove her home from any gathering.

They were, however, lovers, stealing kisses, caresses and meaningful glances at every turn. They made love at Saquish Street with abandon during lunch or when he persuaded her to stop for breakfast on her way in to the station.

One Saturday when Ryan and Sky were in Boston at her family's Beacon Hill house, they joined them for dinner. Megan adored the elegance of the city and Jody ached to end the evening with Megan on the second floor, but both thought better of it. Love was a word she used with increasing frequency but there was nothing between that had tested it.

Alone in bed every night, his frustration grew. He wanted more than the status quo, but he didn't want risk. Already irritable, Jody's temper and his attention span shortened considerably. His packed schedule had barely run smoothly without the likes of Megan O'Connor in his life. He couldn't spare the time to dwell on the state he was in and, yet, he could think of little else.

When he took her sailing, he tried to concentrate on the boat. When they dined, he talked about the food. He took pride in her achievements at the radio station and helped her devise public service programs suited to the south shore.

The month was flying by, their passion refused to die, but never did he hold her all night as he had the very first time. On the pretext of introducing Megan to local cultural events, he asked her to a Friday night concert of the Plymouth Philharmonic Orchestra. His brothers had season seats on either side of him, but at least he was picking her up and taking her home. It gave him a legitimate excuse for his Porsche in her driveway, and when the evening arrived—finally—he took the stairs up to her apartment two at a time.

She greeted him in a sedate, quilted bathrobe, but her voice gave her away. "I thought you'd never get here. How much time do we have?"

"About half an hour."

Megan smiled, suddenly shy. "Jody?"

He led her into the bedroom.

She was wide-eyed, flushed, and her hands trembled but she took his and pressed them to the small covered buttons at her throat. By the time he had unfastened the last one, she had pulled away his jacket and tie.

"Megan?" was a whisper. He stepped back, his breath catching.

She was in a slip, a pale, gauzy bit of lamplight with nothing beneath but everything he ached for. "Incredible." They were on the bed; this time he took her hands in his. He was out of his shirt, his pants, coaxing her, seized by memory.

"Talk to me, Megs." He could barely hear himself over the rush of his pulse.

"I'm happy," she gasped.

"Thank goodness." He slid the fabric above her hip, meaning to play. *Now*, drummed through him, *now*.

Her face brushed his. She welcomed him and the sensation was electric in its speed and depth. Over his own cries, her voice reached his ear. "I love you," Megan whispered, "Jody, I love you."

They were late for the symphony and had to endure the curious glances of one O'Connor and four Branigans as they were seated after the opening piece. Jody hardly heard a note.

So this was what Kevin had found in Erin, what each of his older brothers had found. The possibility of complete joy had dropped into his life like ripe berries off the fall vines. He stole a glance at Megan and she flushed.

In the seats on either side of him were the guiding forces in his life. He loved them all, wanted their approval, sought their direction, but it wasn't enough. Contentment, which had eluded him for so long, was finally his. He felt it, sensed it and finally knew not only where he was going, but how he was going to get there. Megan was just the beginning.

The orchestra continued to play and Jody continued to philosophize. The other voice, the swimmer coming up from the depths, was about to break through to the light and fill his lungs.

After the concert, Jody mingled with his brothers. "I'll be out tomorrow," he told them. "I want to help with the pump house."

"I thought you were going sailing," Ryan replied.

"It can wait."

Kevin shook his head. "If you don't want to work, then for Pete's sake, sleep late, take Megan sightseeing. We can manage. You owe yourself a rest, Jody."

"I'll be there. It's important."

Kevin eyed him and looked at the others before he responded. "If this has anything to do with that night at the sprinklers—"

"Kevin, this has to do with my life, my *own* life."

"Your own life is pretty darn perfect."

He waved them away, too self-satisfied to chance ruining his mood. "Good night. I'll see you guys at the bogs."

"I'd like to go sailing," Megan said as they left the others and headed for his car.

"You will, but tomorrow I've got to work with them."

"They don't seem to need you, Jody. Take their advice. Get some rest."

"Megan, darling, I've been taking their advice all my life."

She looked bemused. "It hasn't done you any harm. Look where you are, thanks to them."

They were at his car, in the recesses of the parking lot. Gently, he pressed Megan back against it and put his arms around her. The kiss transported him, as he knew it would.

She laughed. "What's gotten into you? Every time I looked over tonight, you were grinning like the cat that ate the canary."

"Was I?"

"I don't think you heard a note."

"I was listening to my own music." He kissed her again. "Our music."

"And is it sweet?"

They drove through Millbrook, past Schuyler House and up to the carriage house. "It's nice not to be driving myself home, for once," Megan said.

"It's nice to have a legitimate reason to be here," Jody replied as he walked her to the door.

"I have some brandy, or tea or coffee. Do you have time to stay for a drink?"

Once inside, Jody nodded. "It's time I stayed all night."

Megan looked dreamy eyed. "And you know I'd love you to."

"Then I will."

Alarm. "Jody? We've already—"

"We've already made love tonight so there's no need for me to stay? There *is* Megan, there *is* need. I'm sick and tired of pretending there's nothing going on. It's made my life even more chaotic."

"And what about mine?"

"What about yours? What about yours and mine? I'm tired of lying alone in bed every night and waking up in the morning with the extra pillow crushed at my chest. I'm tired of waiting for this—what did you call it weeks ago—this *initial rush* of feeling to go away. It's not going to go away. You know it and so do I."

"When would you leave?"

"Are you suggesting I sneak out of here before dawn, as if we're doing something illicit?"

"What about Ryan and Sky? What if Sean's on duty? I thought you cared about privacy as much as I do."

"Not as much as I care about straightening things out. I'm at a breaking point. You know it as well as I do. We either stop making love, force this rush to end, or we go on. Can I believe what you've said? Do you really love me?"

She nodded.

"Then I'm staying in Millbrook and you're staying in my arms, all night. I'm the same size as half my brothers and in the morning I can borrow work clothes from them."

Her face was flushed. "You mean you'd go out to the bogs in that suit?"

Jody laughed at her expression. "Give my brothers some credit. Don't you think they know what's going on? Don't you think they've been in my position? Don't you think Erin's been in yours?"

"It's a fishbowl!"

"Darn right and it's my fishbowl."

Twenty

Jody showed up at the bogs just after eight o'clock. The last week of May was seasonably warm and there'd been enough rain to bring much of the foliage into bloom. He parked his Porsche next to the truck. Ryan's Bronco was in the courtyard, as well. He went into the barn and got his boots, leaving them on the farmer's porch as he entered the family kitchen.

Except for Matt, they were all there. Erin was at the table with her saltines. Kevin, Ryan, Drew and Sean were splitting the last of some cranberry muffins. They were all in well-worn pants and faded shirts, ready for heavy manual labor.

Down to the last man they looked him up and down. The dreaded heat crawled up from his dress shirt. "Kevin, I'll need some jeans. I'm here to work on the pump house."

Ryan pointed at him with his muffin, the picture of non-nonchalance. "Didn't I see you in that getup last night, with Megan?"

Drew elbowed Ryan. "It's about time somebody knocked his socks off. The guy's been all work for too long."

"So's Megan, for that matter," Erin threw in.

Jody eyed them all. "I could have driven back into Plymouth to change but I was banking on a little maturity."

His brand new sister-in-law grinned. "I've been wondering how long it would take till you got around to mentioning *entanglements*. I guess you took my heart-melting lecture seriously. Is my sister with you?"

Jody scoffed. "I wouldn't subject her to the facial expressions of any one of you."

Kevin laughed. "Erin's been right all along. I never would have thought, you, of all people, Jody. Must be awfully serious for you to risk showing up in such incriminating evidence."

Jody started for the staircase. "Kevin, none of you may know me as well as you think you do." He left them long enough to pull on his brother's jeans and a faded polo shirt and then came back down for his boots.

He put up with the teasing and the reprimands about his overworking. Being with them felt right, as right as anything else in his life. Half a dozen times he tried to broach the subject of joining them permanently, but the timing was off. In the end, he decided to leave them all with the feelings still swelling his chest.

He knew better than to expect Megan to show up. She'd kissed him goodbye with the excuse of working at the station, unwilling to undergo the anticipated teasing at his semiformal arrival. The teasing would have done her in. There was time for that, too. Time for everything.

When they all finished it was well into the afternoon. And when his brothers asked about his upcoming evening Jody just grinned.

"Love at last?" asked Drew.

"Damn straight," he replied.

Jody left the bogs and went back to Saquish Street, but this time he changed into casual clothes and threw some extras into the car. He picked up groceries and got back to the carriage house before Megan. He had dinner going as she came in.

Megan kissed him. "A pleasant surprise! Manual labor seems to agree with you." She took off her jacket. "Forget I said that!"

The twinge in his chest made him do just that.

They stayed home, ate, watched television and talked about an upcoming interview Jody'd arranged for her with the harbormaster. His heart was brimming.

When they were in bed, in the moonlight, Jody settled next to her. "I love you, Megan. You bring me a peace I've never known. I'd like to believe there's a future in this."

"I think there is. I wouldn't have believed it a month ago, but there is."

"You'd be happy here, professionally?"

"In Boston, eventually. Maybe I'll work my way into the major networks there. We can live on Beacon Hill and come down here for summers, the way Sky did as a child. Maybe you'll wind up in the statehouse, the way Kevin has planned."

His heart thundered, but not from passion. "Megan, if you love me, then it's time to listen to me."

"I love listening to you. You know that."

His palms were clammy. "You and I . . . you're what I want in a woman, but the rest of my life . . . It's time to put the rest of my life together, too."

She sighed against him. "Then will you listen to your brothers and back off from hanging around out there? I would have loved to have been on the bay with you this afternoon."

"There'll always be time for the boat," he replied too quickly. "I'm not just *hanging around* out there. My brothers have it backwards, darling. I want to leave the firm. I want to resign from Hammell, Price and Bennett and work with the bogs."

In the dark, he heard her gasp. Megan reached for the light. "Jody, you're serious! There are smarter ways to deal with pressure than to turn your back on your career!"

"Megan, I've thought about this for a year. If you love me, you must know that who I am won't change. It won't matter that I'm not representing the law firm." It sounded lame, even to his own ears. Of course it mattered. "Who I am won't change," he repeated.

Alarm and confusion darkened her eyes. "Who you are! Jody, it's foolish. Don't throw your life away."

"The life I'm living is killing me, Megan. The only peace I can find is when I'm with you. You've made me a different person. You've made me feel how good things can be. The rest won't come easily—"

"Kevin and the others—"

"They know how I feel. They're smart men. They won't face it until I force it on them, but once I've made them understand, they'll accept it. My question is, Megan, will you?"

She didn't answer and his heart sank. "Megan?"

"You've given me a lot to think about."

"I'm not asking you to marry me. I'm asking you to accept the change now and stay in the relationship. Help me work through this."

She closed her eyes. "I'm still working through my own changes."

He turned off the light and settled back with her. "Sleep on it."

Megan was quiet, tense. "How could you turn your back on everything your family's sacrificed for you?"

"Ironic, isn't it. Kevin thought you were in the enemy camp, and here you are agreeing with him."

She lay stiffly against him without replying and finally he drifted off.

Things fared no better in the morning. They both pulled on casual clothes. Megan brushed out her hair and looked at him. "If I talk, you'll think I'm terribly spoiled. I sound selfish, even to myself."

He read in her face what she couldn't say. He spoke for her. "I think while I turn everybody inside out with my news, you and I should cool things off. Megan, I, of all people, understand your confusion." Pain deadened his words. "I'll need to concentrate on family for a while and you'd get the short end of the stick."

She blinked, hard. "Jody, if you'd only told me in the beginning."

He smiled through the ache. "From the beginning I've told you more than I've ever told another human being. You're like a second skin. You're my sounding board."

"Yes, but this . . . Jody, you've known how I felt all along, about farming, about the bogs, about the kind of life I want."

"Dirt under my fingernails just doesn't suit you. Maybe that's why I didn't say anything. I should have told you but I was the selfish one. Deep down I knew how you'd react. You've always been honest about your feelings. I'm the one who hasn't. I've been quiet for too long, for Kevin and Drew's sake first and now for yours. I always did the right thing because I loved someone. Guilt shouldn't have anything to do with love. I've been living a lie for too long."

She came to him. "Isn't there anything I can do to make you change your mind? Won't you think it over?"

"I have, for a long, long time. I know I'm losing you because of it but it's better now than later, when months, years have gone by."

"We shouldn't have gotten in so deep."

"But we did. Don't regret what's passed. It's been the best thing that ever happened to me, Megan. You've started my life over."

"I didn't want to! Not like this!"

He smiled, touched her face and left the carriage house.

The next morning was sunny, breezy, a perfect day to be on the water. Instead, Jody left the carriage house and drove back to the homestead. Beyond the lawn of Kevin's house sat the five acres of bog fed by the pond bordering Sean and Anne's. The pump house, at the water's edge, was an easy walk, but Kevin had driven the truck out to deliver the lumber, shingles and nails needed for its repair.

The Branigans had already stripped it of the rotted framing and worn-out roof. As Jody stopped at the courtyard, he watched them. Kevin, Drew, Sean and Ryan all helped unload the truck bed and fill it back up with the debris.

There was a beast in Jody's chest he couldn't call grief but it was the ache of loss that made him hurt, loss of the woman too good to be true. Damn his impetuousness. Damn his recklessness and damn his hormones.

He walked over the cart path towards the pump house, kicking up dust with the toe of his boot, and then began to work beside his brothers, silent, mental conversation eating at him like an ulcer.

"Leave your suit at the carriage house this morning, or did you bring along a change of clothes last night?" Sean teased.

"Shut up!"

One identical twin glanced at the other.

"Must be love," Ryan muttered. "I recognize the symptoms."

"I'm here to work, all right?"

Ryan raised both hands in supplication. "All right."

He wanted to sit them down, talk sense, but as long as he kept silent, he still had Megan. The pain refused to quit.

The day grew warm and Jody stopped long enough to strip off his shirt and splash icy pond water over his shoulders. The shock made his chest ache and he pressed his breastbone with his right hand, opening and closing his left fist.

"You all right?" Kevin asked.

Jody looked back at his brother. "Sure. Hot, that's all, maybe some indigestion. I shouldn't have wolfed down breakfast."

Sean grinned. "Maybe cranberries don't agree with you."

Jody scowled. "Cranberries agree with me fine."

Kevin looked at both of them. "I don't want you out here to begin with. Yesterday was more than enough. If it's stress giving you a hard time, then quit right now. We can get along fine without you."

"Don't you think I know that?" he snapped.

Kevin lowered his voice and came to him. "Is it Megan? Surely you knew we'd tease you after showing up yesterday in Friday night's suit."

"Damn it, why does it always have to be a woman if there's a problem? Megan's fine."

"If there's no problem with Megan then why aren't you with her now? Look at this day, Jody. What are you doing wasting it on this construction when you could be with her out in the bay?"

"I'm not wasting anything!" He stood tall, his green-eyed gaze focused on Kevin. "This is what I want. All of you..." His chest hurt and he pressed it again. "I want out."

Twenty-One

——

By now he had everyone's attention. "I want out of the firm. I want out of law." He swept the acres with his arm. "This is what I want. What you have."

Their expressions ranged from annoyed to incredulous. "You want to quit being an attorney? Give up environmental law?"

"Yes." The hollowness was hot.

Kevin brushed his damp forehead with the back of his hand. "Hell of a thing to drop on us in the middle of this."

"You've known it was coming. There's no good time. I tried to tell you the night we monitored the sprinklers. I've tried in a dozen ways," Jody replied.

Drew stared at him. "A slap on the back and congratulations don't seem real appropriate. Look, Jody, I know you've been under a lot of pressure. The week in New York and the wedding and all the work on our

Taft project threw a monkey wrench into your schedule. Okay, it's been tough, but don't give up what really matters. You've worked so hard. *We* worked so hard. Things will get back to normal. They always do."

"I don't want normal. I don't have any feeling for it anymore."

"Feeling!" Ryan began to steam. "Since when are you supposed to have a love affair with your career? You think I *love* spending my nights out here babying cranberries? Do you think I have feelings of affection for repairing this pump house on a gorgeous Sunday?"

"Yes! Ryan, you of all people ought to understand. You came back to it. You were a cop and you quit for something you loved, something that means more."

"Jody, I wasn't a full-time officer. I was an intermittent, a P.I., not a career man. You know good and well why I took the job in the first place."

"Of course I do. It's branded in my brain: for me, for Matt."

Drew pointed in the direction of the equipment barn. "This *career* could have killed Kevin and me the year we fell off the top of the conveyor ramp. You're being selfish. Selfish and crazy."

"I know this is a shock. I know it hurts. You've all sacrificed. Every one of you raised me on noble sacrifices."

"What's that supposed to mean?"

"It means I was never able to tell you that I had doubts. I did what was expected and I know I made you proud. I love you for it, I appreciate everything, but I've never been allowed to choose."

"What the thunder kind of choice did we have?"

Jody looked at his oldest brother. "I shouldn't have brought it up out here. It's hot, we're all exhausted, but it's been eating away at me. Not just this week, but for months. A year, maybe. Maybe more."

"And all the sacrifices?" Drew pointed at Ryan. "His lousy hours as a cop, taking every detail he could for overtime pay?"

"Don't you think I feel guilty about this?"

"No! Not if you're telling us you want to pack up your briefcase and pull on a pair of waders instead."

"This is exactly the reaction I expected from you, Drew."

"Good, then I haven't let *you* down."

"That was below the belt."

"So's your news."

Jody turned his head. "Nothing's come easy for you, Ryan. I thought you might understand."

"Jody, you're talking about a major change in your life, giving up years of expertise, throwing away years of sacrifice."

"Do you have to keep tossing that in my face?"

"I meant *your* sacrifice! Think this over, please."

"Don't you think I have?"

Kevin stepped in. "Frankly, I don't see how you could have and still come up with this conclusion."

Jody sighed. "This isn't getting us anywhere."

Drew looked at Kevin. "Talk some sense into him."

"Can't you see that's the problem?" Jody demanded. "All of you have been *talking sense* into me all my life. From day one I was told what path to follow. First it came from Peter who'd always explain what a tough time Drew and Ryan were having. 'Don't make waves. Don't make things harder for Kevin. He has his hands full,' I was always told." He stopped abruptly.

"There was more to it than that!"

Jody nodded. "God, yes. I was a great student with a sterling future. But it wasn't my future. It was all of yours. Somehow I was to go out and do what you guys couldn't. I wanted to believe it was the right thing, the right path."

"It still is," Kevin replied. "This is stress talking. Can't you see that? I should have noticed well before this. You're burning yourself out."

"No kidding."

"We agree on that, Jody, but the answer isn't leaving your law firm. Where's your common sense? You shouldn't be out here in the heat and you shouldn't be knocking your brains out over the Taft property. We'll set things straight. Just promise me you won't do anything stupid."

"Stupid was trying to make you understand."

"Go home. Go get Megan and take her sailing."

"I'm not a kid anymore, Kevin. I don't need an endless set of directives from you."

"Has she got anything to do with this?"

Jody laughed sardonically. "Would you take me seriously if I told you that I had to give her up to do this? We talked all night. She wants no part of a cranberry grower in her life."

Jody turned away from all of them to try and clear his head but she was there, across the bogs at the edge of the lawn. Megan was on the cart path with Erin, out of earshot, but walking toward them, the dogs at her heels.

The sun caught her hair. Megan.

Frustration contracted into tension and then—*pain*. Jody gasped as a ring of fire strangled him. His pectoral muscles strained against the beast in his chest but when he tried to inhale, it felt like his ribs had splintered, cracked over a knee like so much kindling. He sucked at air. He was hyperventilating but still couldn't get enough air and he gasped until he was light-headed. The searing pain wouldn't stop.

"Jody!" Megan was beside him, her hand flat over the rock-hard muscle spasm, flat over the pain.

The Branigan faces blurred, paled in blinding light that fractured into stars. He needed water and he pivoted. He stared at the twins and couldn't tell them apart.

"Drew," was the last thing he said as he pitched forward against the solid wall of his brother's chest.

The day passed quickly for all of the Branigans, lost in the siren of the ambulance, hours at Plymouth General Hospital, an EKG and what amounted to a complete physical exam.

His heart was fine but he was released with a lecture about hypertension, stress, choices and lifestyle. The physician left him to his heap of clothes. Jody dressed and from the emergency area, he went back into the waiting room and found only Megan. She stood up immediately, obviously shaken. "Kevin sent the others home and then I shooed him away after he'd talked with your doctor."

"No mean feat."

"I had to promise to bring you directly to his house."

"I suppose that's where I ought to go, anyway."

"Unfinished business?"

"We have a lot of talking to do."

"Jody, I'm so sorry."

He looked into her troubled face. "You and I rushed, Megan. Maybe I was afraid you'd disappear. I was being selfish, looking out for my own needs. You filled a void so fast it made my head swim. Once I realized what had been missing, I just kept examining the rest of my life. Whatever we had was wonderful and you made me take a good hard look at myself.''

"It might have killed you.''

"Nah. It should have happened sooner. I'd have spared everybody a lot of trouble. I'm going to get myself on the right track. I'm just sorry it's not the one you want to be on.''

Her eyes filled and the bright blue irises swam in tears she tried not to shed. He watched as they caught in her lower lashes and hung suspended before sliding down her cheek.

He didn't dare touch her. "I love you, Megan. I thought it was the real thing but nothing that's supposed to be love can hurt this much.''

She blinked and nodded. "We gave into the rush.''

"Chemistry?''

She laughed ruefully. "I guess I was right after all.''

They drove back into Millbrook in silence and he thanked her when he got out of the car at Kevin's. Exhausted, drained and sobered by the experience, Jody went into the living room. Erin threw her arms around him and Kevin, the least demonstrative of them all, yanked him into a bear hug. After his wife had left the room, he pulled up a chair.

"You scared the bejesus out of me, Jody. I've invested too much to lose you to stress. I guess it's time I listened.''

And it was time that Jody talked. Without the heat of anger or frustration, he mapped out his life and presented his case to his jury of one.

Jody's week was as full as any had ever been. He sat down with the senior partners of his law firm and walked them through the crisis. He saw each older brother in turn and made them listen one by one. Because Matt was back in Boston in the final weeks of medical school, the consensus was to spare him temporarily from the latest family upheaval.

Plans, work and dreams of the future filled Jody's waking hours. Night after night, when he'd finished, he'd stumble into his dark bedroom. Without bothering to turn on the light, he'd strip to his shorts, leave his clothes where they dropped and fall into his empty bed. His exhaustion and the focus on his professional life kept him from dwelling on the condition of his personal one. He went back to living without love, but he was not living well without it.

June broke through and Jody decided he needed time aboard *Respite*. The day was bright and breezy and he packed a cooler and his gear and drove to the yacht club. In no hurry, he tinkered aboard the catboat while in the slip, then came topside to pull the sail cover back from the mast. Megan O'Connor was walking along the pier in khaki shorts and a simple polo shirt. She wasn't dressed to torment him, but watching her move did just that.

Jody sat down and waited. She looked anxious, less than comfortable. When she reached the boat he said, "Come aboard."

"Erin told me you'd be here."

"So I am."

"I want to tell you something. It deserved more than a phone call. I—we—haven't talked since the hospital."

How well he knew that.

"How are you feeling?"

"For the most part, better than I have in years."

"For the most part?"

"I'm putting my life in order, Megan. It makes me feel good. I'm sure Erin's told you all about it."

Megan shook her head. "No. She says it's your business and I'm to hear it from you. All she'll discuss are names for the baby. James III is at the top of the list."

He arched his eyebrows. "Her idea, maybe. Certainly not my brother's."

"Still giving him a hard time?"

"Depends on your point of view. You'd think so."

"Then you're leaving Hammell, Price and Bennett?"

"Yes, July first."

"To grow cranberries?" The tone of her voice made him wince.

"I'll be growing cranberries. I'm buying into the business. What was your news?"

She looked at the mainsail still lashed to the mast. "I requested a transfer, Baltimore or Chicago."

"How soon?"

She shrugged. "They can't guarantee anything. Since I just got here, it'll probably take a while, even if something does open up. I think it's for the best."

"Seems pigheaded to run away and start all over again. Do you have friends or family in either place?"

"No. Pigheaded!"

"Leaving town because of a man isn't pigheaded?"

"Isn't it what you want me to do?"

"Take it from me, Megan, 'First to thine own self be true.' Otherwise you're not worth a load of cranberry hulls to anybody else."

"This isn't my town."

"Maybe not yet but you have family here. What's Erin's opinion of all this?"

"We don't see eye to eye on much."

"She thinks you're pigheaded, too."

Megan laughed. In spite of the tension and the pain, she smiled at him and he smiled back. "Lord, James Branigan, the first time you smiled at me like that, it turned my knees to jelly."

Why wasn't he backing away from the flame? Where was the pain in his chest? Why the thunder all over again? "I have more where that came from. Megan, tell me truthfully, what do you want? Are the choices I've made for my life so terrible that you can't stick around and at least share the town?"

"Could we share it?"

"If you mean could we go back to being friends, maybe. It would be better than not seeing you at all." He brushed back his hair. "Tell me what you want."

She was wistful. "One last sail."

"Right now, in case they ship you to Chicago Monday morning?"

"You don't mind . . . after everything?"

"Even though we're no longer lovers?"

She winced. "Even though things are different."

Before she had time to change her mind, Jody started the small outboard auxiliary engine and freed the mooring lines from their cleats. As they left the anchorage, a calm settled between them while they concentrated on getting under sail.

Jody had her hoist the main and adjust the gaff rigging while he killed the engine and caught the port breeze. With a rush, they took the wind and meandered out of the channel and into the bay, too late to turn back. There was enough breeze so that he needed her beside him . . . for balance, he told himself.

"You're getting damn good at crewing. I'll miss it." His remark made her expression change. Megan seemed to dissolve only to regain her composure.

Jody sailed the boat across the bay, and after an hour's worth of sea talk and skimming along the shallows of Clark's Island, he nosed *Respite* toward a marshy inlet. He set the anchor while Megan furled the sail. "We make a good team," he remarked.

"I take orders well," she answered.

"Some."

"I meant on a boat."

She looked beyond him, out at the peaceful ripple of the eelgrass and the distant boats, but Jody found only turmoil in her face. He touched her arm. "Megan, what are you doing out here? Why did you come with me?"

Her eyes were wide. "A feeling."

"Try putting it into words. You were always better at that than I was."

"I can't stop loving you." She looked at him through lowered lashes and started to laugh. "You're usually blushing, but Jody, now you're pale."

The blood had drained from his face. "You don't want to love me."

She nodded. "I know that, but I don't seem to be able to do anything about it. I was afraid to bring it up, afraid you'd turn me away. After all you've been through, I thought—"

"Stop analyzing it to death and tell me what you feel!"

"Love, Jody. It never stops. It's making me miserable and I know Chicago or Baltimore or the North Pole won't change it. Neither will the fact that you're going to grow cranberries."

"I may have to sell the Porsche. I may even move back into Millbrook. It's a fishbowl."

"I'm growing to love the town."

"Then stay. Take this one day at a time, Megs, one night at a time. Don't make promises you can't keep, but don't run away from what feels right. I want you with me. You're the only woman I've ever loved."

"We'll fight."

"Branigans do that."

"You'll probably make me put on waders and work during the harvest."

He grinned that grin. "An old farm girl like you would take to it naturally."

She leaned against him and sighed. "Jody, I love you so much. I just can't believe that you'd give up your license—"

"Giving up? I'm quitting the firm, not the practice of law."

"But you're going in with your brothers."

"True. The manual labor's good for my magnificent body. But we mustn't forget about my magnificent mind."

"I don't understand." Her eyes were glistening again.

"It's simple. I'm also hanging out my own shingle: James D. Branigan, Jr., Attorney-at-Law. Growers need legal advice all the time, Branigans and all the others."

"Why didn't you say something?"

"You either love me or you don't. I'm still going to be monitoring bogs in the middle of the night and tearing shingles off rotted pump houses." The relief on her face made him laugh.

"Was this Kevin's idea of a compromise?"

Jody smiled at her. "Mine and Holly's. She's the business end, the brains behind the bogs. You know those Branigan women, a little education and they take over the whole outfit. It might be worth staying in town just to see how things work out.''

"Do you want me to stay?"

"Let me show you how much." He pulled her into his arms and stopped kissing her only long enough to go below. They slid the hatch cover shut and stretched out on the berth. The breeze died, but there in the cove, the boat still rocked gently on the incoming tide.

*   *   *   *   *

Look for Matthew Branigan's story—
PRIVATE PRACTICE—coming in March from
Silhouette Desire.

SILHOUETTE *Desire*

COMING NEXT MONTH

#529 SHILOH'S PROMISE—BJ James
November's *Man of the Month*, Shiloh Butler, was a dark, brooding man. He'd sworn to protect his friend's widow, Megan Sullivan, from danger—but who would protect her from him?

#530 INTERLUDE—Donna Carlisle
A Rocky Mountain blizzard forced wealthy adventurer Alan Donovan and practical schoolteacher Pamela Mercer into close contact. Though they were dependent on each other for survival, surely *these* two opposites couldn't attract.

#531 ULTERIOR MOTIVES—Laura Leone
Ross Tanner looked awfully good to Shelley Baird. He was suave, charming and debonair. But that was before she realized he worked for her language school's major rival!

#532 BLUE CHIP BRIDE—Audra Adams
If Janet Demarest married Ken Radnor, he'd get her stock, she'd get her money, and then they'd get the marriage annulled.
Simple . . . until Ken decided he wanted a great deal more. . . .

#533 SEEING IS BELIEVING—Janet Bieber
Optometrist Lynda Fisher was far too busy for romance—especially with someone like Kent Berringer. But when she opened her eyes she realized that Mr. Wrong was actually Mr. Right!

#534 TAGGED—Lass Small
Another Lambert meets her match. For Fredricka Lambert, Colin Kilgallon had always been just a good friend. But lately, he'd given a whole new meaning to the word "friendship."

Indulge a Little, Give a Lot

To receive your free gift send us the required number of proofs-of-purchase from any specially marked ''Indulge A Little'' Harlequin or Silhouette book with the Offer Certificate properly completed, plus a cheque or money order (do not send cash) to cover postage and handling payable to Harlequin/Silhouette ''Indulge A Little, Give A Lot'' Offer. We will send you the specified gift.

Mail-in-Offer

OFFER CERTIFICATE

Item:	A. Collector's Doll	B. Soaps in a Basket	C. Potpourri Sachet	D. Scented Hangers
# of Proofs-of -Purchase	18	12	6	4
Postage & Handling	$3.25	$2.75	$2.25	$2.00
Check One				

Name _____

Address _____ Apt. # _____

City _____ State _____ Zip _____

ONE PROOF OF PURCHASE

To collect your free gift by mail you must include the necessary number of proofs-of-purchase plus postage and handling with offer certificate.

SD-1

Harlequin®/Silhouette®

Mail this certificate, designated number of proofs-of-purchase and check or money order for postage and handling to:

INDULGE A LITTLE
P.O. Box 9055 Buffalo, N.Y. 14269-9055

NOTE THIS IMPORTANT OFFER'S TERMS
Offer available in the United States and Canada.

A heartwarming tradition continues as Silhouette brings you its fourth enchanting collection of seasonal stories....

Silhouette Christmas Stories 1989

Four of your favorite authors have crafted for you unforgettable and heartwarming stories that glow with the magic of Christmas across the country:

Marilyn Pappano • THE GREATEST GIFT
Lass Small • THE VOICE OF THE TURTLES
Bay Matthews • A CHRISTMAS FOR CAROLE
Brittany Young • SILENT NIGHT

Rediscover the wonder of falling in love as you indulge with Silhouette Christmas Stories 1989. Give this edition to a special friend, as well!

Available in November

Desire

MR. OCTOBER

MAN: Jody Branigan
RELUCTANT MISSION: To unleash the full force of his Branigan charm on unsuspecting Megan O'Connor.
UNEXPECTED SNAG: Megan's own irresistible attractions—bewitching baby blues and a body that wouldn't quit!

If he hadn't been browbeaten into it by all five of his brothers, Jody never would have agreed to their crazy scheme. He couldn't help it if Megan was dead set against her sister's marrying into the notorious Branigan brood. What was he supposed to do to change her mind?

But when she breezed into his room—unannounced—Jody lost his heart to the beguiling redhead. And that was when wooing—and winning—Megan became his "mission possible!"

ISBN 0-373-05523-4